DEVIL'S PLEA BARGAIN

David Brunelle Legal Thriller #11

STEPHEN PENNER

ISBN 13: 9780578613000

Devil's Plea Bargain

This is a work of fiction. Any similarity with real persons or events is purely coincidental. Persons, events, and locations are either the product of the author's imagination or used fictitiously.

Joy Lorton, Editor.
Cover design by Nathan Wampler Book Covers.

DEVIL'S
PLEA BARGAIN

Devil's Bargain *(n.), also: devil's own bargain:*
An extremely bad deal, with a terrible price to pay, which someone considers accepting because they can see no other way out of a truly horrible situation.

Dictionary of American Colloquialisms

CHAPTER 1

The wicked weren't the only ones not getting any rest. The people who pursued them could get pretty sleep-deprived too.

"Why do these callouts always happen at o-dark-thirty?" asked David Brunelle, career prosecutor with the King County Prosecutor's Office. He shoved his hands into his pockets and tried to blink away the puffiness that came with answering a 2:00 a.m. phone call, pulling himself out of a warm bed, and driving twenty minutes to meet a homicide detective over the body of a dead prostitute. Or what was left of her, anyway.

"Nothing good happens after two in the morning," answered the homicide detective, Larry Chen, a twenty-plus year veteran of the Seattle Police Department. "That time is reserved for stuff like this."

And places like this, Brunelle thought. Behind an abandoned pet food warehouse in Seattle's White Center neighborhood.

White Center was the southernmost part of Seattle, far from the glass skyscrapers and tech company H.Q.s that fueled the Emerald City's buzzing downtown. It was separated from the city's retail and financial core by miles of docks, railyards, and warehouses—the things that actually kept a city working, even if the well-heeled tech workers to the north and east didn't want to have to think about them. And beyond those working warehouses were the warehouses that weren't working anymore. The ones that were just a little too far away, a little too far south, a little too grungy—and not in the classic Seattle way. It was there, where U.S. Route 99 changed its name from Seattle's West Marginal Way to Tukwila's International Boulevard, that street-walking prostitutes took their johns to earn enough money to eat and buy the drugs they needed to forget about what they needed to do to earn enough money to eat and buy the drugs they needed. Abandoned warehouses and empty lots were the perfect place for a fifteen-minute, $20 "date".

Unfortunately, it also made the perfect place for some bastard to keep his $20, murder his date, and dump her remains where no one was likely to find her. At least not right away.

Brunelle knew the victim had been a prostitute. Not because of what was left of her clothing—almost a costume, grotesquely ridiculous with its short plastic skirt and impossibly high stilettos—but by the very fact that it had taken so long to find her. The flesh on her face, neck, and one shoulder was completely gone, replaced by an undulating mass of fly maggots. Brunelle knew that meant the fatal trauma had been inflicted somewhere in there, but it would take a forensic entomologist to determine exactly how long since that fatal blow, as calculated by the average life cycle of the local fly species times the number of generations that had been laid on, hatched on, and fed by the body.

Oh, the things you learned prosecuting homicides.

The other thing you learned doing homicides was that prostitutes made the best murder victims—if the only thing the killer was interested in was the pure rush of killing another human being. The typical murder was either a domestic dispute fueled by years of familiarity, anger, and hatred, or a random encounter fueled by alcohol, drugs, and testosterone. Those were one-offs. The husband is always the prime suspect, and the gunfight in the bar parking lot has a hundred witnesses. But if you were in the murder game for the long run, victim selection was key.

"Do we have a name yet?" Brunelle asked, even though he knew the answer.

"No," Chen answered as expected. "There was no purse or I.D. And her face is, uh…"

"Gone," Brunelle observed.

"Yeah." Chen nodded. "We're gonna have to do dental records."

"How'd the body get found?" Brunelle asked. "Some kids throw their ball too far?"

Chen laughed darkly. "Kids don't play ball around here, Dave. Especially not at two in the morning. No, one of the Dobermans guarding a nearby junkyard dug under their fence. Came back with an arm bone. There was enough cartilage left for some of the carpal bones and a couple fingers to stay attached too. The night watchman called 9-1-1."

Brunelle thought for a moment. "Did we get the arm back? It's evidence."

"I didn't ask," Chen answered. "But I'm guessing you're going to have to prove the case without that particular piece of evidence. You ever try to take a bone away from a Doberman?"

"I'm going to need a defendant before I can prove anything," Brunelle remarked. "Any suspects?"

Chen shook his head again. The two men were having their entire conversation while keeping their eyes trained on the half-gelatinous remains in the brush at their feet. "Not yet. But once the bug doctor pinpoints the time of death, we can start asking people questions. Maybe somebody saw something. Maybe we get a lead. Maybe we find the bastard who did this."

Brunelle shrugged and looked around the abandoned cityscape they found themselves in. "You think so?"

Chen thought for a moment, then sighed. "No."

CHAPTER 2

That perfect murder victim was perfect in part because she was forgettable. Already forgotten by family, quickly forgotten by friends, even forgotten by the cops who were supposed to be finding her killer. And if not by them, then definitely forgotten by the prosecutor the cops were planning on handing the case off to once they captured the suspect.

A few weeks after that 2:00 a.m. callout to White Center, Brunelle was sitting at his desk on the 9th floor of the King County Courthouse in downtown Seattle, working on one of his dozens of other, actually solved cases. His thoughts were interrupted by the ringing of his phone. It was Chen.

"Three names," the detective said after initial greetings.

Brunelle didn't know what Chen was talking about, but he was willing to bite. "Okay."

"Jack Forbush," Chen said. "Ashleigh Engel. Michael James Kincaid."

Brunelle waited a moment, but there was no more. Just the names.

"The new lineup for Channel Three news?" Brunelle

guessed.

"Witness, victim, suspect," Chen answered.

Brunelle hesitated. "Which case again?" Those names weren't familiar at all.

"The bug lady down in White Center," Chen reminded him. "The bug doc pegged the time of death at fourteen to sixteen days before the body was found. We pulled the shift schedules and security video of every business within two miles of the dump site. Jack Forbush works the graveyard shift at a used tire lot just up the road. He said he was standing out front taking a smoke break when he saw a car come flying out of the gravel lot next door and head north on West Marginal. He didn't think much of it at the time, but we watched their surveillance video. The camera on the side building caught the car pulling into the lot and disappearing behind the warehouse before coming out again about ten minutes later. The camera in the front caught the license plate as it sped past."

"So, Ashleigh Engel is our victim?"

"Right," Chen confirmed. "Dental records were conclusive. Twenty-eight, lengthy criminal history."

"Let me guess," Brunelle knew. "Drugs and prostitution."

"Mixed with the occasional assault and resisting arrest," Chen expounded. "Definitely still living the lifestyle."

"And the license plate?" Brunelle prompted.

"Returned to one Michael James Kincaid," Chen said.

"White male, mid-forties, no criminal history," Brunelle ventured.

"Exactly," Chen confirmed. "With a current address on both the vehicle registration and his driver's license. We're scooping him up right now. Wanna watch the interrogation?"

Brunelle let himself smile, despite the subject matter. Or maybe because of it. "I wouldn't miss it. Meet you at the precinct."

CHAPTER 3

The 'precinct' was the Seattle Police Department Headquarters at 5th and Cherry downtown. The interrogation room was in the basement. And the suspect, Michael James Kincaid, looked like a total jerk.

Brunelle was watching from the adjoining observation room. No two-way mirrors anymore. Just a video feed from a camera in the corner of the ceiling. It made for a weird fish-eye angle, but there was no mistaking the calm, psychopathic grin on Kincaid's smarmy face. Brunelle hated him already. Which was actually a good thing, since Brunelle's job would be to put Michael James Kincaid in a cage for the rest of his life.

For his part, Kincaid couldn't have looked more relaxed. He was the picture of a middle-aged white guy. His head was essentially bald, closely shorn to hide the male pattern baldness that would otherwise have left a crown of hair around his ears and the back of his head. He wore a dark hoodie over a light T-shirt. Dad jeans and big brown shoes completed the look of someone you wouldn't look twice at.

He was leaning back, an arm dangling casually over the

back of his chair. He was looking around, but not nervously. There just wasn't really anything else to do. And even that only revealed the door the patrol officer had locked behind him, and the surveillance camera at the ceiling. Kincaid's gaze stopped at the camera. He smiled, but didn't wave. He didn't need to.

"That's our guy," Chen announced as he entered the observation room to check in with Brunelle. "What do you think?"

"I think he looks like a dick," Brunelle answered. "But he also just looks like somebody's kid's football coach. I would have preferred someone more murderer-y."

"Murderer-y?" Chen repeated. "Is that a word?"

"Did you understand what I meant?"

"Yeah."

"Then it's a word." Brunelle frowned and looked back to the monitor. "He's guilty, though, so that's something."

Chen looked at the image of Michael James Kincaid. "Why do you say that?"

"An innocent person would be freaking out," Brunelle opined. "But this guy? He knows exactly why he's here."

Chen didn't argue. "Good. That will make this go quicker. You need anything specific?"

Brunelle scoffed. "A full confession would be nice, but I won't hold my breath. Still, I'd like something more than just a license plate. Box him in. Get the concessions I need. Put him there. Don't let him claim someone else was driving his car that night. Don't let him say he was there for some other reason, then he saw someone else dumping a body, so he got scared and sped away. He may not admit to the murder, but get him to admit to everything else. His car. He was the driver. No one else there that night. Do that and I can carry it the rest of the way across the goal line."

Chen clapped him on the shoulder. "I'll see what I can do."

Brunelle frowned at the detective. "That doesn't sound very confident."

Chen looked again at the monitor. "Like you said, he knows exactly why he's here. That usually either means a full confession or nothing at all. I'll try to avoid the nothing at all."

"Good plan," Brunelle quipped. He looked again at the reclining figure of Michael James Kincaid. "And good luck."

Chen departed and it was only a few seconds before Brunelle watched him walk into the interrogation room and sit down opposite Kincaid.

"Mr. Kincaid," he started. "I'm Larry Chen. I'm a detective with the Seattle Police Department. I'd like to talk with you about one of our open investigations."

Good start, thought Brunelle. Just because they both knew why they were there didn't mean either of them had to admit it. It was a dance. A dance in the dark where someone keeps moving the furniture, but a dance nonetheless.

"Would you be willing to talk with me?" Chen asked.

Kincaid smirked, still in repose on his plastic chair. He took a beat before answering, "Of course, Detective."

Chen nodded. "Great." He took out a card from his shirt pocket. "Now, I just need to advise you of your constitutional rights. Standard practice. You understand?"

Kincaid finally sat up. "Yes, Detective. I understand."

So Chen went ahead and read out the rights advisement from his department-issued card. When he finished, he asked the question also printed at the bottom of that card. "With these rights in mind, are you willing to answer my questions?"

Kincaid smiled again, and waited even a little longer before nodding. "Yes, Detective."

"So, Michael," Chen started, slipping the card back into his pocket. "Can I call you Michael?"

"Sure, Detective," Kincaid replied coolly.

"Great," Chen said. "Do you know why you're here, Michael?"

"Yes," Kincaid answered. "I'm here because you had me arrested."

Chen smiled slightly at that. "Do you know why we arrested you?"

It was a classic interrogation technique. Get the subject to incriminate himself, admit they know what they did. But it worked best on subjects who were nervous, or at least remorseful. Kincaid wasn't giving off either of those vibes.

"Because you think I committed a crime," Kincaid answered.

Ball, Chen's court. Brunelle frowned slightly. It already wasn't going well.

"Do you know what crime?" Chen kept trying.

But it wasn't going to work. "Why don't you tell me?" Kincaid suggested with a grin.

Chen chewed on his cheek for a moment, clearly deciding what to try next. "So, you like prostitutes, huh?"

Kincaid took a beat before replying as well. Several beats in fact. He was sizing up Chen, his eyes scanning the man opposite him, the gears in his head turning. "You're a detective," he said finally. "You're old, too. Late middle age anyway. That means you're likely toward the top of your department's hierarchy. You handle major crimes, felonies at a minimum. But patronizing a prostitute is a simple misdemeanor." Kincaid shook his head. "No, you're not wasting your time on a prostitution charge."

Chen nodded. "You're right. I'm not. But I'm going to ask the question again. You like prostitutes, don't you?"

Kincaid narrowed his eyes. "Even if it's just a misdemeanor, I'm not likely to admit to it, Detective. Why would I do that?"

"Because it's a lot less serious than why you're really here," Chen answered.

"But not unrelated," Kincaid returned. "Or you wouldn't have asked the question."

Brunelle frowned a little deeper and crossed his arms. It was taking too long. Kincaid was playing.

Chen seemed to think so too. He switched gears. "You drive an Audi Quattro. Used, but still a nice car. You've had it for almost three years now. How do you like it?"

Kincaid grinned again, almost a sneer. "Am I supposed to be impressed that you can access Department of Licensing records, Detective? Yes, it's a nice car. I like it fine, thank you."

"I can access surveillance video too, Michael," Chen continued, unperturbed. "I know you were driving on West Marginal about four weeks ago. I know you stopped behind the old PetMax warehouse. And I know you drove away pretty damn fast for someone who's acting so cool right now."

Kincaid didn't have a comeback ready. *That was progress,* Brunelle supposed.

"It also coincides," Chen continued, "with the time of death of a woman named Ashleigh Engel. Do you know a woman named Ashleigh Engel, Michael?"

Kincaid just shrugged. "Probably. I know a lot of people."

Weak, Brunelle thought. *Good*.

"Let me make it clearer for you, Michael," Chen pressed. "Do you know a *prostitute* named Ashleigh? Because that's whose body got dumped behind the PetMax warehouse at the exact same time your very nice used Audi Quattro was caught on video speeding away from the dump site."

Kincaid didn't answer. There were any number of excuses for why his car might have been identified. Maybe the surveillance video was grainy and the cops got the license number wrong. Maybe the time of death wasn't as exact as Chen was making it out to be. Maybe he could claim someone else was driving his car, someone he barely knew and couldn't locate now of course.

Kincaid's dilemma was that he had less information than Chen. He didn't know how clear the video was. He didn't know if the video also showed the driver to be a bald white male. He didn't know whether the body had been discovered immediately or the time of death had to be estimated based on, say, the average lifespan of a fly. If Kincaid guessed wrong, he was signing his own guilty verdict.

Chen decided his subject needed a little encouragement. "And we don't need surveillance equipment to get a license plate number, Michael. Sometimes we run sting operations. Sometimes we put a decoy out on West Marginal Way and take down the plates of all the cars that stop and talk to the girls there. And sometimes we notice when one of those girls leaves in a nice used Audi Quattro and never comes back."

Kincaid just blinked at Chen.

Brunelle blinked too. That bit about the prostitution op was made up. A gambit. A lie. Cops were allowed to do that actually, despite what a lot of criminals thought. Brunelle just hoped it would work.

"I'm going to get a warrant to search that car of yours, Michael," Chen continued. "Every last nook and cranny. We'll use Q-tips to swab every crease and seam. Tell me, Michael, do you think we're going to find any of Ashleigh Engel's DNA in your Audi Quattro?"

Kincaid took several seconds before answering. He didn't smile, but he shook his head confidently. "No, Detective. I don't think you will."

"Why not?" Chen shot back. "Because you cleaned up afterward? Or because you took precautions beforehand?"

Kincaid's smile arrived. "You're the detective," he grinned. "You tell me."

"I will," Chen answered. "After we search your car."

"Why are you bothering to search my car, Detective," Kincaid leaned back in his chair and opened his palms to his interrogator, "if you already think you have enough evidence to arrest me?"

Chen could smile too. "It never hurts to collect more evidence."

"But if you search and find nothing," Kincaid posited, "isn't that evidence I'm innocent, notwithstanding your grainy surveillance video and alleged sting operation?"

Chen hesitated. Brunelle frowned.

"Look, Michael," Chen deflected, "we both know two things. You murdered her, and I'm going to prove it."

Kincaid laughed lightly. "You aren't going to prove anything, Detective. That's the prosecutor's job, in court. And quite honestly, if this is all you have, I'm not sure he's going to be able to do it either."

"Is that so?" was all Chen could muster to throw back at

Kincaid.

Brunelle raised a worried hand to his chin.

"Yes, it is," Kincaid answered. He leaned forward onto the table between them. "But don't worry, Detective."

Chen hesitated, but then went ahead and asked. "Why not?"

Kincaid smiled broadly, his grin cold and mirthless. "Because I promise, Detective, when I get out—and I will get out if that's all the evidence you have—it won't be long before I give you another reason to try to catch me."

Chen slammed a fist down on the table. "Now, you listen here, Kincaid—"

"I'd like a lawyer now, Detective," Kincaid interjected calmly. He nodded up toward the camera in the corner of the ceiling. "I assume that prosecutor I just mentioned has been watching this whole time. It only seems fair I have a lawyer as well."

And with that, the interrogation was over. Chen couldn't ask any more questions once Kincaid said the magic word, 'lawyer.' Well, he could, but Kincaid's answers wouldn't be admissible in court, so there was no point.

But that didn't mean Chen actually had to provide a lawyer. He just had to stop asking questions.

"You can talk to your lawyer at your arraignment," Chen barked.

"Splendid," Kincaid answered. "May I go to my cell now? Or is your case so thin that you actually have to release me right now?"

Chen's grin returned. It was rueful. "Don't worry, Michael, we have a cell ready for you. And you better get used to it. If I have anything to say about it, you'll spend the rest of your life in it."

"I'm guessing the lawyers will do a lot more talking than either of us, Detective," Kincaid replied, "but it was nice to chat with you. Good luck with the search of my vehicle."

Chen tried to stare Kincaid down, but it had zero effect. So, he stood up and stormed out, leaving it to the patrol officers to transport Kincaid to that aforementioned cell in the King County Jail. Brunelle watched as the two young officers entered the interrogation room and took custody of Kincaid. Kincaid was perfectly compliant. On his way out, he looked up at the camera one last time and mouthed a kiss at the unknown prosecutor watching him.

He'd know Brunelle's name soon enough.

Chen pushed open the door to the observation room and walked in almost as calmly as Kincaid walked out of the interrogation room.

"Not sure that prostitution sting op ploy worked," Chen started. "It seemed like that's when I lost him."

Brunelle nodded. "I think you're right. But it's okay. If he knew you were lying about that, it's because he knows how he really picked her up that night. It actually confirms he's the killer."

Chen laughed slightly. "Nice spin, counselor." Then he pointed toward the image of the empty interrogation room on the observation monitor. "He's a tough one, I'll give him that."

Brunelle looked at the monitor as well. "That's okay. I know someone tougher."

CHAPTER 4

"Gwen Carlisle, on behalf of the State."

Brunelle's prospective co-counsel introduced herself for the record on the hearing she was just beginning in Judge Martinez's courtroom. She was a decade younger than Brunelle's mid-40s, but had already established herself as a tenacious litigator. One of the best in their office. She dressed the part too. Dark suit, all business, light blonde hair cut sharply just below her jaw. When she walked into a room, everyone knew who was in charge.

Even a mostly empty courtroom, like Martinez's was just then. Contrary to what was depicted on a lot of prime time courtroom dramas, most criminal cases were sparsely attended, if at all. There were just too many of them. Thousands a year in every county in every state all across the country. Only the most interested people on the most interesting cases would bother showing up for anything other than the actual trial. Certainly not a preliminary procedural motion like Carlisle was about to argue.

So, when Brunelle entered the courtroom just as

arguments were starting, he was beyond conspicuous. The judge looked up from his notes to see who had entered his courtroom. The bailiff and court reporter glanced his way too. Even the defense attorney and the defendant swiveled their heads to see who had dared and/or bothered to interrupt their hearing.

The only one who didn't turn to look at him was Carlisle. She simply proceeded.

"We're on today for the defendant's motion to sever counts for trial," she announced. "The State opposes severance and filed its brief seven days ago, as required by the court rules. This is a defense motion, so the defense will argue first, but we are prepared to respond as to why severance is inappropriate and these crimes should all be tried together before the same jury. Thank you."

With that, she sat down and finally stole a glance back at Brunelle. When she saw him, she surrendered the slightest eye roll, perceptible to Brunelle but not the judge, who was focused on the opening lines of the defense attorney's argument. With a sharp flick of her hand, she gestured Brunelle to come down and join her at the prosecution table. He knew to comply.

"What are you doing here, Dave?" Carlisle demanded in a whisper as Brunelle sat down next to her. "I'm kind of busy."

Brunelle looked over at the defense attorney, who was already sweating and stumbling through his argument, but in a somehow endearing way. Like the judge might take pity on him.

"I can see that," Brunelle replied in his own whisper. "Sorry, I didn't think the hearing would start on time. Martinez isn't exactly the most punctual judge in the county. I thought I could grab you before you started."

"He's getting some kind of civic award tonight," Carlisle said. "The clerk told us to be on time and succinct." She looked over at her opponent, who was still struggling through his argument, heavily embellished with copious hand gestures. "Well, we were on time anyway."

She returned her gaze to Brunelle. "Now, quick. Why are you here? Trying to learn some pointers from the next generation?"

Brunelle forced a polite smile. "I'm not out to pasture quite yet. But if you're willing to work with an O.G., I've got a new case you might be interested in."

"Is it a murder case?" Carlisle asked.

"Yep."

"I'm in."

Brunelle cocked his head at her. "Don't you want to hear about it?"

"Was it actually a murder?" Carlisle asked.

"Yes," Brunelle answered.

"So, the victim didn't deserve it or anything?" Carlisle pressed. "If they did, it would be self-defense or necessity or something else, not murder. But this is a murder?"

"Right," Brunelle assured her. "It wasn't self-defense. The victim definitely didn't deserve it."

"I'm in," she repeated. Then she raised a finger at him and stood up. "Hold on."

"Any response, Ms. Carlisle?" Judge Martinez asked, either oblivious or indifferent to Brunelle's presence at the prosecution table.

"Absolutely, Your Honor," Carlisle replied. "Joint trials are favored, in part for judicial economy, but especially when the evidence in one trial would be cross-admissible in any separate trials. Here, the charges and the evidence are cross-admissible under both the evidence rules and the Sixth Amendment. Importantly, defense counsel's argument rests primarily on *State v. Klemmer*, a 1995 case that has since been all but abandoned by our appellate courts. *Klemmer* was distinguished in 2003 by Division Three of the Court of Appeals, then again in 2010 by Division One. Last year, the State Supreme Court explicitly overruled *State v. Orloff*, the 1988 case upon which *Klemmer* was based, effectively rendering defense counsel's argument devoid of any merit whatsoever. I respect that defense counsel is doing his job by bringing forward a standard motion and hoping for a positive ruling, despite the law. But the Court needs to do its job, too, and enforce that law. The Court should deny the defendant's motion to sever counts and keep all of the charges joined for a single trial. Thank you."

Brunelle nodded approvingly at Carlisle's argument. Concise, coherent, prepared, persuasive.

"Perfect," he admired aloud.

Carlisle sat down again and turned her attention back to Brunelle, even as Judge Martinez started to deliver his ruling in her favor.

"So," she asked, "how weak is this murder case that you had to ask me for help?"

Brunelle had to grin at her insight. "Pretty damn weak," he admitted.

Carlisle smiled too, but broadly. "You're right. Perfect."

CHAPTER 5

Chen found Kincaid. Brunelle found Carlisle. And public defender Jessica Edwards found herself assigned to the case of *The State of Washington v. Michael James Kincaid*, one count of murder in the first degree.

"Good to see you again, Dave, Gwen," Edwards greeted them as they walked into the arraignment courtroom the next afternoon, right after lunch. The court rules gave the State up to 72 hours to file charges, but Brunelle didn't see any reason to wait. "Long time, no trials. Although I think that may change with this one."

Brunelle and Edwards had started practicing about the same time. Their careers had mostly run parallel, both of them cutting their teeth on shoplifts and trespasses, then graduating to lower level felonies like drug possession and car theft. There were diversions, of course. Edwards did a stint in drug court while Brunelle spent some time at juvenile hall. But in criminal law, the corporate ladder leads to homicides, so as they entered the prime of their careers, both Brunelle and Edwards started taking on homicide cases, first as second-chair assistants, then by themselves, and now with their own assistants. Well, Brunelle anyway. Edwards still tried her murder cases alone.

Or not.

"This is Pete Saxby," Edwards pivoted to introduce the young man behind her. "He's going to be helping me out on this one."

Saxby was what they used to call 'a tall drink of water.' He was probably 6'5" and thin as a rail. His suit hung off him like he was a standing wire clothes hanger. A bushy head of thick black hair stuck up over a clean shaven baby face. He stuck out a large, bony hand. "Pleasure to meet you, Mr. Brunelle. Jessica has told me all about you." He turned to Carlisle. "Hi, I'm Pete."

"I'm Ms. Carlisle," she replied, with a jab of her thumb at Brunelle. "If he gets an honorific, so do I."

Saxby just blinked at her.

"You called him *Mr.* Brunelle," she explained. "Mister is an honorific. So, if—You know what?' she shook her head. "Never mind."

"Why don't we just all go with first names?" Brunelle suggested. "I'm not quite ready for the new generation to be calling me Mr. Brunelle. Call me Dave."

"Dave. Got it," Saxby confirmed. He turned again to Carlisle. "And you are...?"

Carlisle stuck out a pouty lip at Edwards. "You told him all about Mr. Brunelle, but nothing about me?"

"I didn't know you were going to be on the case," Edwards defended. "But don't worry. I'll fill him in on everything. Pete, this is Gwen Carlisle."

"Call me Gwendolyn," Carlisle instructed Saxby. "That's my full name."

"Really?" Edwards cocked her head at Carlisle.

"Yep." Carlisle grinned at her. Then, to Saxby, "You have to call me Gwendolyn. But I'm not calling you Peter. Understood?"

Saxby nodded. "Understood."

"Understood, *what*?" Carlisle prompted with a raised eyebrow and roll of her wrist.

Saxby thought for a moment, then ventured, "Understood, Gwendolyn."

Carlisle smiled. "Nice. Yeah, we're going to get along just fine."

Brunelle raised a hand to closed eyes. "Are we done? We should probably get on with the arraignment on that murder thing we're all here for."

He lowered his hand from his face and looked at Edwards. "You said you think this will be a trial? I haven't even made an offer yet."

Edwards smiled. "Your offers suck, Dave. This is going to be a trial. Thin evidence, plus recalcitrant client, equals trial."

"It may be thin now," Brunelle postured, "but wait until the search of the car is finished. The report will probably be on my desk by the time we get back to the office."

Jessica gave a knowing smile. "You won't find anything in the car, Dave."

Brunelle frowned. "Yeah, your guy already told us that."

"He would know," Edwards pointed out.

"Care to share how he's so certain?" Carlisle interjected.

"You know I can't do that, Gwen," Edwards responded. "Attorney-client privilege, professional ethics, bar card, job, mortgage." She shrugged. "Sorry."

"You don't really seem sorry," Carlisle observed. "It

must be difficult knowing someone is guilty but defending them anyway."

"Not at all," Edwards answered. "I don't mind holding the government to its burden. If you don't have the evidence, you shouldn't get the conviction."

"But what if *you* have the evidence?" Carlisle countered. "What if the reason you're so confident there won't be any evidence in the car is because he told you what he really did."

Edwards pasted on a professional, and therefore warmth-free smile. "You have your job and I have mine."

"I'm glad I don't have your job," Carlisle scoffed.

Edwards's smile held firm. "Me too."

The judge entered the courtroom then to a bellow of "All rise!" from the bailiff. It was Judge Edward Carpenter, one of the longer-serving judges. All of the judges took turns doing the criminal presiding court calendar. Arraignments every afternoon all afternoon, and guilty pleas every morning all morning. Pretty mindless stuff, but with ninety-five percent of all criminal cases resolving in some sort of plea bargain, it was where the sausage of the criminal justice system was made. And no one wanted to watch sausage being made. Not all the time anyway, hence the rotation.

Judge Carpenter would be as good as any to preside over the hearing. There weren't a lot of issues at an arraignment. Charges filed, not guilty plea entered, pretrial conference scheduled. The only issue was bail, and no judge was going to set bail at less than a million dollars on a Murder One. It was about as *pro forma* as any criminal hearing could be.

"You wanna handle this?" Brunelle asked Carlisle, handing her the file.

Carlisle looked at the file for a split second. Brunelle

almost expected her to protest. Almost.

Carlisle took the file. "Yes, I do." Then, after another second, "Thanks."

Brunelle looked over at their opponents. Edwards laughed lightly and shook her head. "Oh, no, Mr. Brunelle," she said. "I'm handling this myself. Pete is learning, not driving."

Saxby looked both sheepish and a little relieved. Brunelle filed that away. They might both have assistants, but that didn't mean they were both going to have help.

"The parties are ready, Your Honor," Carlisle had already stepped up to the bar to call the case, "on the matter of *The State of Washington versus Michael James Kincaid*. The case comes on this afternoon for arraignment on one count of murder in the first degree."

That drew the appropriate amount of hushed whispers and sudden silence from the other lawyers gathered in the courtroom. Most arraignments were property crimes and drug offenses, with the occasional assault or other violent crime to keep things interesting. But murders were, mercifully, relatively rare. Still, they were the top of that ladder they were all climbing without ever stopping to consider whether it was really the right destination for them after all.

"Jessica Edwards appearing on behalf of the defendant, Mr. Michael Kincaid," Edwards stepped forward to announce her presence as well. Now all they needed was that defendant.

Judge Carpenter nodded to the corrections officer at the secure door to the holding cells just off the courtroom. The officer opened the door and shouted inside, "Kincaid!" A few moments later, Kincaid shuffled into court. His hoodie and jeans from the interrogation had been replaced with red jail scrubs. His big brown shoes replaced by rubber slip-on sandals. His freedom replaced with handcuffs and leg chains connected to the belly chain threaded through his belt loops.

But he still had that cocky grin as he made his way, with some difficulty, to his spot next to his attorney. Edwards placed a quick hand on his shoulder. "Hello, Michael," she tried to sooth him. But he didn't really look like he was interested in being soothed. He scanned the courtroom, but only the part that affected him. Edwards and Saxby, Brunelle and Carlisle, the judge and bailiff and court reporter, with a final check over his shoulder to confirm there was a guard standing within grabbing distance. "Ready?' she whispered.

Kincaid thought for a moment. "I don't suppose it really matters, does it?"

Edwards shrugged. "No, not really."

"Have you received a copy of the charging documents, Ms. Edwards?" Judge Carpenter asked. "And would you waive a formal reading?"

"I'd rather not waive anything, Your Honor," Kincaid interjected.

"I'm sure you wouldn't," Carpenter replied quickly. "But you should speak with your attorney before making any further statements."

Brunelle took note. Maybe Kincaid was more impulsive than he'd seemed during the interrogation. Maybe being locked up was starting to get to him already. Maybe he hated letting someone else be in control. Probably all three. In any event, it was good for Brunelle.

Which is why Edwards was, at that very moment, Brunelle knew, telling Kincaid to shut the hell up and let her do her job.

She looked up at the judge. "I've explained to Mr.

Kincaid that the Court was simply asking if he would waive a formal reading of the charges out loud in open court. Now that he understands that, yes, we will waive a formal reading and ask the Court to enter a plea of not guilty to the charge."

Brunelle glanced over at Kincaid to see if he was having trouble letting someone else speak for him. But to his surprise, and disappointment, Kincaid suddenly looked as relaxed and confident as he did when across the table from Chen.

Judge Carpenter turned to Carlisle. "I'll hear first from the State regarding conditions of release."

"Thank you, Your Honor," Carlisle responded. "The State is asking the Court to set bail at two million dollars. We would also ask for law abiding behavior, no contact with the family of the victim, and travel restricted to King County. Thank you."

Kincaid wasn't going to post two million, Brunelle knew, so the travel restriction was probably unnecessary. But even in jail you could break the law again or make a phone call to the victim's family. Then again, the victim didn't really have any family, not any that cared about her anyway. That was why she ended up being Kincaid's victim.

"Ms. Edwards?" Judge Carpenter prompted a response from the defense.

"Two million dollars is excessive, Your Honor," Edwards argued. "Mr. Kincaid has no criminal history whatsoever. He has lived his entire life in the Seattle area. He owns a home here and has had the same job here for over ten years. He is not a flight risk, Your Honor."

"Flight is only one consideration, Ms. Edwards," the judge reminded her. "The other consideration is risk to the community."

"As I said, Your Honor," Edwards responded, "Mr. Kincaid has no prior criminal history. Nothing more than traffic tickets in all the time he's lived here. And I'm sure I don't need to remind the Court—"

Which meant she was about to remind the Court, Brunelle knew. So did Judge Carpenter.

"—Mr. Kincaid is presumed innocent," Edwards continued. "That means it would be inappropriate to consider the facts of this case to decide whether he poses a risk to anyone in our community."

Carpenter offered a bemused smile. "You don't think I can consider the fact that he's charged with killing someone when deciding whether he poses a risk to anyone?"

"Correct, Your Honor," Edwards insisted. "He is presumed innocent. Under the law, he no more committed this crime than did I. Or Mr. Brunelle. Or Your Honor."

Judge Carpenter didn't seem to appreciate being lumped in with a murder defendant. Or maybe it was being lumped in with Brunelle. In any event, he wasn't buying Edwards's argument.

"The Court will set bail as requested by the State," he ruled. "Two million dollars. The Court will also impose the other conditions recommended by Ms. Carlisle."

And that was the hearing.

"Thank you, Your Honor," Carlisle said.

Edwards echoed it. "Thank you, Your Honor."

Kincaid piped up again. "Yes, thank you, Your Honor."

What a jerk, Brunelle thought.

Then, as they stepped away from the bar and the corrections officer laid hands on him, Kincaid shot a leer behind Edwards's back. "And thank you, Miss Carlisle."

Carlisle narrowed her eyes at him. "Don't talk to me, dirtbag," she growled, but softly enough the judge wouldn't hear.

Edwards was just realizing what was happening when Kincaid let out a low whistle. "Oh dear, such bad manners from such a pretty lady. Well, don't worry," he whispered at her. "I know how to handle women who think they're strong."

CHAPTER 6

"He knows how to handle strong women?" Casey Emory, Brunelle's girlfriend and a detective with the Bellevue Police Department across Lake Washington from Seattle, nearly spit out her wine. "Did he actually say that?"

"Yep," Brunelle confirmed. He was nursing an Old Fashioned while they waited for the waiter to come and take their orders. Saturday night in Seattle's Belltown neighborhood. It had taken forty minutes just to get a small table by the bathrooms. They could hardly expect faster service once they were finally seated.

Brunelle didn't mind. He and Emory hadn't been dating that long, so he hadn't done whatever he was going to do to screw up their relationship yet. He could just enjoy her green eyes, brown skin, and soft curls. And her company, of course.

"What did Gwen say?" Emory asked. "Did she excoriate him?"

Brunelle grinned. "No. She's not one to yell back at someone. Not without it being exactly what she planned. She just stared at him for a few seconds while Jess was trying to figure out what was happening. Then she pointed at our copy of the charges and waved 'Buh-bye' to him."

Emory laughed. "Did she actually say 'Buh-bye' like that?"

"Yeah, it was pretty awesome." Brunelle nodded. "I picked the right person to co-try the case with me."

Emory shook her head and took another sip of her wine. "I'll show him a strong woman," she grumbled. "A strong woman with a gun."

"And a badge," Brunelle cautioned. "So, don't go over to the jail and shoot him in his cell or anything. You might lose the badge for that."

"I should get a second badge for that," Emory scoffed. "And a ribbon. Maybe even a sash. Definitely a promotion."

"A sash?" Brunelle laughed. "You don't seem like a sash girl."

"I'm a sash *woman*, Dave," she corrected. "Don't you ever forget that."

She took another drink of wine, then her expression turned serious. "You're going to take him down, right? Somebody like that needs to be locked away forever."

Brunelle didn't disagree, but he could only shrug. "I hope so. It's a pretty thin case actually. Totally circumstantial. Chen couldn't get him to confess. In fact, Chen lied to him and told him they were running an undercover prostitution sting and saw the victim get into his car that night, but I think he knew Chen was lying. He was starting to get nervous at that point, but then got all cocky again and asked for a lawyer."

Emory frowned. "Overreach."

"Yeah," Brunelle agreed. "And when he reads through all the police reports and doesn't see anything about any undercover prostitution op, he's going to know it was a lie. Then he's really gonna smell blood."

"I'll make him smell blood," Emory growled. "His own, when I break his nose."

"Okay, really, calm down," Brunelle half-laughed. "I'll get him. No need to go all vigilante. I mean, it's kinda hot, but people are starting to stare."

Emory frowned, but didn't argue. "This is going to screw up our vacation plans, isn't it?"

"What, that weekend on Whidbey Island?" Brunelle confirmed. "No, I think we're good."

"Long weekend," Emory clarified. "And I can see that look in your eye. You're worried."

"First of all," Brunelle raised a cautionary finger at her, "I don't have looks in my eyes. Second, of course I'm worried. This guy is a psycho. I need to hold him responsible. Chen's given me everything he can. I just need to make sure it's enough.

"Did they search the car?" Emory asked.

"Yeah, but it came up empty," Brunelle answered. "No DNA matches. There were trace amounts of DNA in the passenger compartment and even the trunk, but none of them matched our victim. He told us we wouldn't find anything, and he was right. Edwards told us the same thing, actually, at the arraignment."

"That's because he killed her in a different car," Emory said.

"What?" It was Brunelle's turn to nearly spit out his drink. Which would have been a shame. It was a really good Old Fashioned.

"That's how he knew Chen was bullshitting him about

the prostitution op," Emory explained. "And that's how the defense attorney knew you wouldn't find anything in the car you seized. He picked her up and killed her in a different car, then used the one you have to dump the body, just in case he was seen. Easy enough to keep DNA out of a car if the bleeding has stopped and you wrap the body in plastic."

"There was no plastic around her body," Brunelle told her.

"Then you lay the plastic down in the trunk and dispose of it afterward," Emory replied. "Either way, he knew what he was doing."

Brunelle nodded and took another thoughtful sip of his drink. "So, we just need to find that other car."

Emory laughed. "Yeah, good luck with that. It's not like he's going to call you up and tell you where his murder-mobile is."

Brunelle's phone rang then, buzzing on the table in front of him. It was Jessica Edwards.

Brunelle answered the call. "Hey, what's up, Jess? You know it's Saturday, right?"

Emory scanned the restaurant for the waiter. Her glass was empty.

"Yeah. Uh-huh," Brunelle was saying. "Okay. Sure. Uh, right now? Um, yeah. Sure. I mean, give me an hour. Well, I gotta get ahold of Chen, so maybe two. Right. Okay. See you then."

"Forget our vacation," Emory laughed. "This case is already screwing up our dinner, isn't it?"

Brunelle set his phone back down on the table. "Kincaid wants to talk," he said. "He has an offer for us."

CHAPTER 7

Chen answered on the first try. He acted unsurprised, as if he'd expected Kincaid to give him a do-over on the interrogation. It was Brunelle who was surprised. Not so much that Kincaid wanted to talk. Control freaks always want to talk; they think they can talk anybody into anything. No, Brunelle was surprised Edwards would let Kincaid talk at all. First rule of Defense Attorney Club is don't let your clients talk about Defense Attorney Club, or anything else.

The meeting was set at the jail, not Seattle Police H.Q. You don't transport accused murderers, even just a few blocks, and even though there was video recording equipment at the H.Q. that they just didn't have at the jail. All it would take was one overturned bus and suddenly the defendant would be running through a sewer tunnel to find the man really responsible for his wife's murder. No, no risks. If what Kincaid had to say was worth anything, they could always make arrangements to have him say it again later and record it then.

That meant a cramped conference room inside the jail. It was designed for a one-on-one meeting between an attorney and a client, not an attorney, her client, two prosecutors, and a detective. But they would have to make do. Kincaid sat at the table. Edwards stood behind him. Saxby wasn't there; Saturday night proffer statements were big kid territory. Saxby could stay home playing video games. Chen sat opposite Kincaid again, with Brunelle and Carlisle standing behind the detective, arms crossed, skeptical but curious.

Even though Chen was going to be asking the questions — so he could be called as a witness later if necessary — he wasn't in charge anymore. Charges had been formally filed, so the lawyers were in charge now. They had called the meeting. They would determine the parameters of the statement. They would decide the import of whatever Kincaid might say.

Which betrayed that the lawyers weren't really in charge either. Kincaid was. And he loved it.

Brunelle, not so much.

"Okay, we're here," Brunelle barked at Kincaid once the jail guard closed the door to the conference room behind them. "Spit it out."

"Before my client says anything," Edwards interjected, "we need to be in agreement that this is a statement made for the purposes of negotiations. That makes it inadmissible against him under Evidence Rule 408."

Brunelle pursed his lips. "You called us all in here for him to say something that could never be used against him? Kind of feels like that could have been an email."

"We're not here to give a confession, Dave," Edwards responded. "This is an offer. You have to agree that anything he says can't be used against him."

"I can't make that broad of a promise, Jess," Brunelle said. "I mean, maybe I could agree to that as to anything he says about this case, but what if he suddenly confesses to a bunch of other murders?"

Edwards's expression told Brunelle he'd just hit the nail on the head.

"Oh my God, Jess," Brunelle gasped. "Really?"

"You have to agree, Dave," Edwards repeated. "Nothing he says can be used against him."

"I should have known," Brunelle shook his head at himself. "You don't kill just one prostitute. And, of course, we weren't lucky enough to catch him after the first one." He looked Edwards in the eye. "How many?"

"Dave..." Edwards was still arguing the inadmissibility issue.

"How many, Jess?" Brunelle demanded.

"A lot," Kincaid piped up. "Enough to make it worth your while to listen to me."

Brunelle glared down at Kincaid, still calm and smug in his plastic jail chair. "What do you want, Kincaid?"

"I want a deal, Prosecutor," Kincaid replied evenly. "I want to get out of prison again before I die. I want a Murder Two."

"Murder Two?" Brunelle repeated even as Carlisle laughed out loud at the suggestion. "You want us to amend the charges to one count of murder in the second degree? That's like ten years, plus five for the gun."

"No firearm enhancement," Kincaid insisted. "Murder two, no enhancements, low end of the range."

"You want ten years total for killing 'a lot' of people?" Carlisle stepped forward. "Why the hell would we ever do that?"

"Because I can lead you to those other bodies," Kincaid explained. "I don't know who they were, because I don't care, but I know where their bodies are. I can help you solve those cases, bring closure to the families, and all that. Let everyone move on again."

"Including you," Carlisle spat. "No thanks."

Kincaid frowned at her, then looked up again at Brunelle. "I see your assistant doesn't appreciate the value of my proposal, but perhaps you do, Prosecutor?"

"I'm not his assistant," Carlisle growled.

Kincaid ignored her. "What do you say, Prosecutor? Do we have a deal? Nothing you do can bring any of those women back. But you can do something to bring peace of mind to a lot of families."

"Every time you say 'a lot'," Brunelle said, "I'm even less inclined to make a deal with you."

"Don't think about those other cases, Dave," Edwards put in. "Think about this case. It's paper thin, and you know it. All you have is a license plate. No witnesses, no DNA, nothing. And that story about seeing the victim get into my client's car? We know that's bullshit."

"You know it's bullshit because you know how he really did it," Brunelle pointed out.

"And you don't," Edwards retorted. "But you can. He'll tell you everything. Everything about this case, and everything about a bunch more. He'll plead guilty to murder, Dave. He'll go to prison. It's a win-win, and we can both move on to our next case."

"It's not about the next case, Jess," Brunelle replied. "It's always about the case right in front of you."

"So, take the conviction, Dave," Edwards practically pleaded. "Plus, solve a whole bunch more. You'll be a hero."

"A hero for giving a serial killer ten years?" Brunelle

scoffed.

"A hero for putting a murderer behind bars," Edwards countered. "No one will care how much time he gets."

"I'll care," Brunelle protested.

"Well, perhaps that's your problem," Kincaid spoke up.

Carlisle pointed at Kincaid but addressed Edwards. "Tell your client to shut the fuck up right now."

Edwards didn't like the tone, but she knew Kincaid wasn't helping. She put a hand on his shoulder and looked to Brunelle. "Why don't you guys step outside and discuss it? Maybe you'll see some value to our offer."

Brunelle looked around at Carlisle and Chen. They all nodded in agreement. "Yeah, no need," Brunelle announced. "I know I speak for all of us when I say, go to hell."

Kincaid laughed. "Oh, I'm sure I'm already going, Prosecutor. But when you lose this case and I walk free, I'll have a chance to get a few more notches on my punch-card."

CHAPTER 8

Brunelle spent the rest of the weekend angry, incredulous, and worried. Angry that his Saturday night had been ruined. Incredulous that Kincaid and Edwards thought he would ever agree to their offer. And worried, because they had a point: his case was paper thin.

When Monday morning arrived, all that anger, incredulity, and worry fueled an early morning bitch session with Carlisle. She was mostly just angry.

"What a piece of shit," she grumbled from where she was slouched in one of Brunelle's guest chairs. "And Kincaid was even worse."

Brunelle laughed despite himself, but raised a hand of caution. "I've known Jess for a long time. She was just doing her job."

Carlisle shrugged. "It's a shitty job, then."

Before Brunelle could disagree—and he wasn't sure we would have disagreed—his legal assistant, Nicole Richards, stuck her head in the door. "What are you two carrying on about? No one should have this much energy first thing on a

Monday morning."

Nicole had been Brunelle's legal assistant ever since he joined the major crimes team and started doing homicides regularly. She'd been working homicides for several years before Brunelle arrived, even though they were approximately the same age, since he'd had to waste seven years in college and law school. She would have excelled as a lawyer, but not everyone had the same opportunities in life. She taught him a lot when he first arrived, and she was a constant reminder to treat everyone well no matter what you think their station in life might be.

"Come in and sit down," Brunelle motioned toward the empty chair next to Carlisle. "You're not going to believe this."

When Brunelle got done explaining Kincaid's offer, Nicole fell back in her chair. "I don't believe it."

"I know, right?" Brunelle said. "We couldn't either."

"What did you say?" Nicole asked.

"We said no," Carlisle answered. "Of course."

"Actually, I think we said, 'Go to hell'," Brunelle corrected.

"You said that," Carlisle clarified. "But that meant 'No.'"

"It also meant he could go straight to hell," Brunelle added.

"Who could go straight to hell?"

All heads turned to the man suddenly standing in the doorway. It was Matt Duncan. Brunelle's boss. And Carlisle's boss. And Nicole's. Everyone's boss. He was the elected prosecutor and everyone in that office worked for him. Luckily, he was a good boss. And a hell of a lawyer too, or so the legends went. He spent his days in conference rooms and campaign events now, rather than courtrooms and crime scenes. But he hadn't forgotten his roots. You don't forget those types of roots.

"Oh, you're gonna love this one, Matt," Brunelle said, again motioning into his office. "Gwen and I have a murder case against this guy named Michael James Kincaid. He murdered a prostitute down off West Marginal Way in White Center. Dumped her body behind an abandoned pet food warehouse. We didn't find her for a couple of weeks until a guard dog dug under the fence and came back with her arm bone in his mouth. Anyway, most of the flesh on her skull and neck was gone, eaten away by maggots. The forensic entomologist pegged the time of death to about two weeks before. The cops pulled some nearby surveillance footage and caught Kincaid's car speeding away from the dump site right when the body was dumped, so now he's charged with one count of Murder One."

Duncan's eyes narrowed. "Okay," he said slowly. "So, what's the part I'm going to love?"

"He wanted to make a deal," Carlisle jumped in. "Turns out that wasn't the first dead prostitute he dumped behind a warehouse."

"He offered to tell us where the bodies were buried," Brunelle explained. "Literally. But get this. In return, he wanted to plead guilty to one count of Murder Two, ten years. Can you believe that?"

Duncan thought for a moment. "How many bodies?"

Brunelle cocked his head. "What?"

"How many bodies?" Duncan repeated. "How many other murders would it have solved?"

Brunelle hesitated. "I don't know," he admitted with a shrug. "We didn't get that far into the negotiations."

"We told him no," Carlisle said.

"Well, that's not exactly what they said," Nicole laughed.

"You said no?" Duncan confirmed. "Before you knew how many cases it could solve?"

"The more cases, the worse it is, Matt," Brunelle protested. "I'm not going to let him use his victims' corpses as bargaining chips."

Duncan took a moment, chewing his cheek and nodding as he looked somewhere well past any of the people in front of him. After another moment, he fixed his gaze on Brunelle. "Can I talk to you for a minute, Dave? In my office?"

Duncan may have been a good boss, but he was still the boss. Brunelle was about to be reminded of that.

CHAPTER 9

"Close the door," Duncan instructed as they walked into his corner office at the end of the hallway.

Brunelle complied, then took a seat across from Duncan at his boss's large, mahogany desk.

"First of all," Duncan raised a cautionary finger at Brunelle, "don't dismiss me like that in front of other people. I value your opinion, Dave, but you better at least act like you value mine too."

"Of course I value your opinion, Matt," Brunelle assured. "You know that."

"Then why didn't you seek it out?" Duncan challenged. "I may not be able to keep track of everyone's cases, Dave, but you need to know when to bring one of them to me. One victim is a you case. A dozen victims is a me case. You have to know when something is bigger than just one more file on your desk, and you have to bring those to me for consideration. You can't just get all jacked up playing Mr. Tough Guy Prosecutor and tell a defendant to go to hell when he might have valuable information."

"Valuable to him," Brunelle grumbled.

"Maybe," Duncan conceded. "But valuable to us too. That's why it's called a deal."

"It's a bad deal, Matt," Brunelle insisted.

"How do you know that, Dave?" Duncan pushed back. "You don't, because you didn't ask. You didn't get specifics. How many? How far back? What would he really be willing to accept? I agree with you: ten years would be too low for multiple murders, but that was his opening offer, Dave. Come on, man. Be smart about it. No one expects to get their opening offer."

Brunelle considered the man he watched Chen try to interrogate. "This guy might."

But Duncan shook his head. "He was expecting a counteroffer. He would take twenty years if it meant he could get out again before he dies. How old is he?"

Brunelle shrugged. "Forty-something, I guess. Maybe fifty."

"Exactly," Duncan slapped his desk. "He pleads guilty to murder, gets twenty years, has a chance to see the sun again before he dies, and we close a dozen unsolved cases. Dave, that's not a terrible outcome."

Brunelle thought for a moment. "It is to me."

"Well, it's bigger than you," Duncan reminded him. "Like I said, that one case, it's yours. But the other twelve? Those are mine."

Brunelle exhaled deeply and put his head in his hands. After a moment, he looked up again. "Don't do this, Matt. Not yet. Twenty years isn't enough. I'll get more than that from this one case."

"Will you though?" Duncan asked. "That summary you

gave me just now—your case sounds pretty thin. You're going to need more than a license plate and a maggot family tree."

Brunelle grimaced. "I know. It is thin. But I think I can use what Kincaid told us to make it stronger."

"But that's just it, Dave. He didn't tell you anything," Duncan pointed out. "You didn't let him."

"But he did," Brunelle countered. "He told me he'd killed more women, a lot more. He told me he didn't care who they were, so they were probably prostitutes too. He told me he knew where the bodies were, which means the bodies are still there to find. We can use that information to solve them without his help. We have a verified suspect now. We can take his DNA. We can cross-reference his home and work addresses for the last ten years against every missing prostitute from here to Tacoma. I just need one more body and I can give the jury two murders to consider. You know he did it the same way. Even if this case is thin, I can use M.O. evidence to link them together."

Duncan pursed his lips. He didn't seem convinced. But he didn't say 'No' either. Yet.

"I can get him, Matt," Brunelle promised. "We don't have to make a deal with the devil."

Duncan again didn't reply immediately. He leaned back in his leather desk chair and drummed his fingers on his desktop. Brunelle knew to shut up and wait.

Finally, Duncan leaned forward again. "Thirty days, Dave. I'll give you thirty days to solve another of those murders and get enough evidence to put that bastard away for the rest of his life. But if you can't do it, then we're accepting his offer."

CHAPTER 10

"Thirty days?" Emory repeated. "Yep, our vacation is screwed."

She had stopped by Brunelle's office to pick him up for drinks and dinner. But he was still at his desk, papers strewn everywhere, when she arrived. Maybe they'd get delivery.

"I wonder if I can get the deposit back," she said to herself, pulling her phone out to look up the place she'd reserved for their getaway.

"I mean, I guess I could probably spare one night," Brunelle offered. But not even half-heartedly. More like quarter-heartedly.

"Spare one night?" Emory laughed. "Oh, Mr. Brunelle, you are so romantic. You really know how to make a girl feel special."

Brunelle frowned. He waved at the mess of case files and crime scene photos spread out between them. "You get it, right? You get how important this is?"

"Of course I do," Emory replied. "I'm a cop. This is what I do for a living. I was just hoping I could forget that for three days and two nights."

Brunelle frowned. "I'm sorry, Casey."

But Casey laughed again and waved the apology away. "Don't apologize for doing your job, Dave. I don't need your pity."

Brunelle blinked at her. "What do you need?"

"I need my deposit back." Emory nodded at her phone, then looked at the case connecting them across his desk. "And I need to help."

CHAPTER 11

"Michael James Kincaid is a murderous psychopath," Brunelle announced, "and we have thirty days to prove it."

His audience was an assemblage of homicide and major crimes detectives from up and down the State Route 99 corridor between Seattle and Tacoma. Cities like Seattle, Tukwila, Burien, Des Moines, and Federal Way were all represented. And Bellevue. Bellevue was a good ten miles northeast of SR 99 and there hadn't been any murdered or missing prostitutes in the uber-affluent suburb—probably ever—but Bellevue Detective Casey Emory sat in the back of the briefing room at Seattle Police H.Q. You don't say 'No' when your girlfriend asks to help you catch a murderous psychopath.

Chen and Carlisle were in the front row. The rest of the dozen or so attendees filled the seats between them. Emory was in the back. Everyone who was invited either showed up or sent someone in their place. Cops liked being cops for lots of different reasons, but all of them would tell you one of the top reasons was catching bad guys. And they didn't come any worse than Kincaid.

"This is the case we've charged." Brunelle pointed to the photograph of Ashleigh Engel taped to the large whiteboard behind him. Then he pointed to twenty-one other photographs similarly taped up across the length of the board, a red line connecting each face to a point on the large map centered in the middle of them. "And these are your unsolved cases."

A slight grumble passed through the room. Cops also didn't like being reminded of their failures. Although, to be fair, no one did. But if those cops were going to have to talk about their unsolved cases, better that conversation be led by one of their own, not some lawyer pretending to be a cop. Cue Larry Chen.

"Larry?" Brunelle nodded to Chen, then stepped away to take his own seat next to Carlisle.

"Thanks, Dave." Chen stood up and took over the presentation. The room palpably relaxed. Chen walked over to the map. He pointed at the red dot connected to the photo of Ashleigh Engel. "Approximately five weeks ago, a night watchman found a half-decomposed body behind the abandoned PetMax warehouse on West Marginal Way in White Center."

"Well, his dog did," Brunelle whispered to Carlisle. She just hushed him, eyes fixed on Chen and the whiteboard.

"Approximately three weeks ago, we arrested Michael James Kincaid for the murder," Chen continued. "And approximately one week ago, Kincaid tried to make a deal with the prosecutors." A nod to Brunelle and Carlisle. Brunelle looked around at the detectives. Carlisle didn't. Just as well; none of them were looking back. "He offered to plead guilty to the murder of Ashleigh Engel if they reduced his sentence to only ten years."

Another grumble rippled through the briefing room. Every one of them had been a cop long enough to have had at least one case where the prosecutor cut a sweetheart deal that had pissed them off. "In exchange, Kincaid offered to give up the location of multiple other murders he had committed, presumably in the same way. To their credit, the prosecutors told him to go to hell."

A general murmur of approval rippled over the room. That was nice.

"But that leaves us with a problem," Chen continued. "Now we know Kincaid committed multiple murders over the last several years. But we don't know how many, and we don't know for how long he's been doing it. I'm going to be honest with you; the case we have against him isn't that great either. We got a license plate from nearby surveillance video, but that's it. He lawyered up and there was no DNA in his car. Without this deal, he might walk on everything, and that's the worst possible scenario."

Nods and grunts of agreement filled the room.

"The prosecutors' boss has given them thirty days to pin one of these other murders on Kincaid," Chen explained, "or he's going to take Kincaid's offer. And we already spent three days getting this meeting organized. We need to move quickly."

A detective near the back spoke up. "What makes you think we can solve a case in twenty-seven days that we haven't been able to solve in two or five or ten years already?"

"Because now we know who did it," Chen answered. "We just need to link him to it."

"How do we do that?" another detective asked. "It's not like we didn't try the first time around."

"The first time around, you didn't know there were up

to two dozen more murders committed by the same person," Chen said. "You stayed in your jurisdiction, did your investigation, and closed the case when the leads dried up. But now we're all here, in the same room, with a verified suspect."

He gestured to the whiteboard. "These twenty-one cases were selected based on three criteria, all of which match the profile for Ashleigh Engel. Every victim was working as a prostitute at the time of her disappearance. Every victim died from trauma to the head or neck. And every body was found within five miles of where Kincaid was living or working at the time." He paused, then pointed toward the three photos bordered by a green circle. "Except those three. Those are missing person cases. Their bodies were never found. But they were last known to be working the streets in the vicinity of Kincaid's home or work. Just because we didn't find the body doesn't mean it isn't out there somewhere."

That answer seemed to satisfy the questioner. "So, now what?" another detective asked.

"Now, we compare notes," Chen answered. "Each of you will brief the rest of us on your case or cases, and we'll look for similarities, something to tie them together, something we may have overlooked before."

"I gotta say something," another detective spoke up. She pointed toward the board. "That's a lot of cases. Some of them he probably didn't do. Especially the missing person cases."

Chen nodded. "You're probably right. And if we can eliminate some of these cases, good. Less cases to try to solve. But we can't eliminate any of them yet."

Chen gestured widely at his audience. "So, who wants to go first?"

Before anyone could answer, Emory interjected from the

back. "No, don't go randomly," she said. "Go in order. If he really did all of these, he would have refined his technique over time. His first attempts were probably pretty amateurish. But he would have learned from his mistakes. We need to look for that pattern too."

Brunelle smiled. They may not have murdered street-level prostitutes in shiny rich Bellevue, but they had a pretty good detective there.

"Good point," Chen nodded. He looked back at the whiteboard. "Okay, first case. Laura Mahoney. Des Moines." He pointed to the two detectives from that particular suburb. "Go."

"Uh, okay," one of them started. He was younger, with a stout cop body, short hair, and a goatee. His partner was older, even more stout, with a bushy mustache but no beard. "I was still on patrol when this one happened. The detective who actually investigated it retired years ago, but we pulled the file and took a look at it."

He took out a series of crime scene photos and held each one up before handing it to the others to pass around. "It was a pretty bloody scene. The medical examiner said she died from strangulation, but she also had a lot of blunt force trauma to her head. Multiple skull fractures, plus scratches on her face and neck. It looks like there was a pretty big struggle, but the assailant had something heavy that he used to bash her in the head until she finally passed out, then he strangled her to death."

"Gruesome," Carlisle whispered. Brunelle couldn't disagree.

"Any chance he left behind some DNA?" Chen asked.

The other Des Moines detective shrugged. "Probably. But whether they knew to collect it, I can't say. It was a long time ago. DNA analysis has come a long way since then."

Brunelle frowned, but nodded. That was true. They used to need a half-dollar size of blood to be able to profile someone's DNA. The days of solving murder from saliva on a drinking glass were still relatively new.

"Any suspects?" Chen continued. "Any witnesses?"

"No suspects," the younger detective confirmed. "And according to the reports, the only witnesses were the girls she was working with the night she went missing. But none of them wanted to make a formal statement, so there weren't really any leads. Honestly, I think the detective who had the case stopped doing any further investigation within forty-eight hours of the body being found. It was just a dead prostitute, I guess. He had no leads and other fish to fry."

Chen nodded. Brunelle wasn't sure if it was because he understood why a detective would stop investigating a murder case after only two days, or it was just to signal moving on to the next case. He chose to decide it was the latter.

"Okay, who's next?" Chen asked, more to himself. He consulted the whiteboard. "Jenny Garrabalino. Six months later. Burien, right across the city line from Des Moines." He turned back and scanned the room for the detectives from Burien.

It was the woman who had spoken up earlier. She raised her hand. "That's me. But I wasn't a detective yet either. All I can go off of is the file." She patted a rather thick case file sitting on the table in front of her. "Our detective didn't give up after forty-eight hours, but he didn't get much further, I hate to admit. Similar situation. Victim was a prostitute working on Pacific Highway, our name for State Route 99."

Brunelle looked at the map. Jenny Garrabalino's body was found just a few miles away from Laura Mahoney's, but in a different jurisdiction. That definitely helped Kincaid avoid detection, as neither agency would know they were dealing with a multiple killer. Brunelle wondered whether Kincaid had done that intentionally or had just been lucky.

"Our victim was shot in the head," the Burien detective continued, "and the neck. Three shots total. Just like the last case, there was blood everywhere. There were no other injuries to her face or neck, but she had powder burns on her hand, likely from grabbing the barrel of the gun during a struggle. Looks like one clean shot to the head."

"So, he did learn," Emory posited.

"If it was him both times," one of the other detectives challenged. They were probably wondering why a Bellevue cop was even there. "We don't know that yet."

Brunelle felt the urge to jump to the defense of his girlfriend, but stopped himself. She could handle herself, he knew.

Emory nodded. "Good point," she admitted. Nothing more disarming than admitting the other person is right.

"But at least possible," Chen resurrected the theory. "We need to keep our minds open to any pattern. Who's next?"

And so it went. Twenty-one missing prostitutes. Eighteen bodies. All dead from injuries to the head. Emory had stood up during the third presentation and started building a chart of relevant facts on the whiteboard. Location of injuries, type of weapon, method of disposing the body, etc. There was definitely a pattern. Improved methods of killing: from a blunt object, to a gun she saw coming, to a single shot in the side of the head. He learned. He got better. And he got away.

Chen took a moment to study the completed chart. From the earlier cases, you could practically predict the exact details of how Kincaid had killed Ashleigh Engel.

"I'd say Kincaid's our man," Chen announced. "But I don't know if we'll have enough to prove any one of them beyond a reasonable doubt."

"We might not need to." Brunelle finally stood up again. "Not individually anyway. If we can link him to even one of these, I can use it in the other case as evidence of how he kills his victims, and get it admitted as *modus operandi*. Each case could fill in the gaps in the other case."

Chen cocked his head. "You think the judge will let you do that?"

Brunelle shrugged. "The evidence rules say I can. Not sure about the Sixth Amendment, but we can let the defense attorney worry about that."

Chen shook his head. "You're such a lawyer sometimes."

Brunelle looked at the map and the crisscrossed red lines and green circles and the photos of twenty-two dead women. "Sometimes that's exactly what you need to stop a murderous psychopath."

CHAPTER 12

Emory had been right: chronologically was the best way to run through the cases. It was also the best way to investigate whether they could link Kincaid to them. Or at least it was one way, and it was the way Brunelle chose. Carlisle and Chen came along for the ride too.

And the first ride was to the property room at the Des Moines Police Department. Des Moines was four cities south of White Center along State Route 99, after Burien, Tukwila, and SeaTac. Tucked between Puget Sound on the west and Interstate-5 on the east, Des Moines had a quaint downtown marina district and a waterfront state park. It also had the site where Laura Mahoney's murdered and 'very bloody' body had been dumped. By Michael James Kincaid. Probably. Hopefully. Or at least Brunelle hoped, in that weird, dark way a homicide prosecutor could hope for something professionally.

That younger detective met them at the precinct—their only precinct. He wasn't actually all that young—he was well into his thirties—but Brunelle was finding more and more people were seeming younger and younger. He tried not to think about it. Instead, he tried to remember the young detective's name as he extended his hand in greeting.

"Thanks for meeting us, Detective uh..." he fumbled.

"Jorgenson," the detective provided. "But call me Rick."

Rick Jorgenson. Brunelle told himself to remember that. He knew he wouldn't.

"Thanks for coming down, guys," Jorgenson said to all three of his guests. "Let's head back to the property room. Linda has everything all set up for us."

Linda was Officer Linda Hamilton, the manager of the property room. Des Moines was a lot smaller than Seattle. They only needed one precinct, one property room, and one full-time property room officer, so she got to be the manager too. But it meant she knew all the cases, especially the unsolved murder that had been taking up space in the back of her property room. She had taken down all the boxes and laid them out in the viewing room for Detective Rick WhatsHisName and his guests from Seattle to pick through, hoping to find something to solve the case and finally clear up some shelf space.

"Here's everything," Hamilton announced as she pushed open the door to the viewing room. "Everything we have left anyway."

Brunelle's heart sank. Already. He was expecting it to sink at the end of their trip, when they hadn't found anything useful, not before they'd even tried.

"What do you mean, what you have left?" he asked.

Hamilton frowned and started pushing at the boxes. "We have protocols for what we keep and what we don't, but those protocols are always changing, especially for biohazard material. This was a murder case, pretty bloody, if I recall. That stuff can only hold up for so long, even refrigerated. Eventually you have to document what you have and get rid of it. I mean, eventually the bacteria is going to get rid of it for you anyway, right? So, you might as well be the one controlling it."

Brunelle nodded understandingly to Hamilton, then turned and shook his head painfully at Carlisle. "So, what about, say, blood samples?"

"Well, more like blood stains," Carlisle corrected. "You didn't have a suspect to take samples from. Although we do now."

"That's what I hear," Hamilton chimed back with a smile. "But I don't know, actually. Let's take a look. Maybe we'll get lucky and there will still be something here for you to use."

She opened the nearest box and started removing items from it. Most of the items were actually envelopes with other items inside, their contents identified by the writing on the outside. When she got to the one marked 'Blood samples', she handed it to Brunelle.

"See?" he chided Carlisle. "Samples."

Carlisle just rolled her eyes.

Brunelle took a pair of latex gloves out of the box on the table and pulled them on. He opened the envelope. Then his heart sank further as he pulled out, not blood samples, but a folded sheet of paper.

He opened the sheet and read it to himself.

"Shit," he hissed. He handed it to Carlisle.

After a moment, she agreed. "Shit."

Chen took it from Carlisle and read it aloud. "Pursuant to property room protocols regarding the retention of biological evidence samples, the blood samples contained in items seven through twelve have been analyzed and identified for blood type and destroyed. The report detailing the results of the blood typing is attached."

"Blood *type*?" Carlisle asked.

"Yeah, like A positive, B negative, O," Brunelle explained.

"I know what it means, Dave," Carlisle huffed. "I don't know why it's useful. Or why you would destroy evidence after doing some rudimentary, Stone Age forensic analysis on it."

"This is an old case, Gwen," Chen said. "They couldn't do DNA like now. Blood typing was the standard back when this evidence was collected. You can't positively identify someone with it, but you can rule people out."

"So, even if Kincaid's blood type matches one of the stains, that doesn't mean he did it, right?" Carlisle confirmed. "It just means he shares the same blood type with the killer, and like twenty-five percent of the human population of the earth."

"Right," Chen admitted.

"And if it doesn't match?" Carlisle continued. "Does that exclude him?"

Chen shrugged. "Depends. It just means he didn't provide the blood that was tested, although that might just be because he didn't leave any blood behind."

"Or they didn't collect what he did leave behind," Brunelle put in.

"It was a pretty bloody scene," Jorgensen reminded them. "I'm sure they didn't collect every drop of blood like they would now."

"Why would they?" Carlisle threw her hands up. "It wouldn't prove anything anyway."

Brunelle nodded toward the report in Chen's hand. "What were the results?"

Chen turned the page and frowned. "They were all B

positive. Including the sample from the autopsy."

"So, it was the victim's blood?" Carlisle asked.

"Or they both have B positive blood," Chen answered.

"That is the most common blood type," Hamilton put in. She smiled weakly. "You learn things doing this job after a while."

Carlisle shook her head. "Well, we didn't learn anything from that report. Is that it, then? The blood samples are just gone? There's nothing to test, no way to connect Kincaid to this murder?"

Chen and Jorgenson took a few minutes to rummage through the rest of the boxes, pulling out more sealed envelopes and examining the writing on them. Once all the boxes were empty, Chen turned back to the lawyers and shook his head. "Nope. Nothing else. Dead end."

CHAPTER 13

Laura Mahoney hadn't been able to help them from the grave. Perhaps Jennifer Garrabalino would have more information to share. But the next day's visit to the Burien Police Department's property room was even less encouraging than the excursion to Des Moines.

"You don't have any property on this case?" Brunelle asked, dumbfounded.

"Are you fucking kidding?" Carlisle gave voice to the subtext of Brunelle's question.

"Everything went with the body to the medical examiner's," explained the property room manager, Officer Elliot Grayson. He looked to be about ten years past retirement, with thin white hair and thick black glasses. "I'm sorry, but as I recall, there wasn't much evidence to collect. It was pretty much just a skeleton out in the woods."

"I thought those detectives gave us details on the case," Brunelle complained to his partner. "How did they do that if there was no evidence?"

"They said she was shot multiple times," Carlisle

recalled. "I guess you could tell that from the bullet holes in the skull."

Brunelle nodded, then pulled out his car keys. "Come on. Let's go."

"Where?" Carlisle asked, although she didn't hesitate to turn toward the parking lot.

"Back downtown," Brunelle answered. "The King County Medical Examiner's Office."

* * *

"Jenny Garrabalino?" asked Jacob Kaladi, the Assistant Medical Examiner who greeted Brunelle and Carlisle and led them from the lobby into the depths of the Medical Examiner's Office. He was old, elderly even, with a frail, bony frame and a slicked back white hair atop his liver spotted head. Brunelle was surprised Kaladi was still working, but some people never retired until they left the office feet first.

"I can't say the name rings any bells," Kaladi went on, "but then again, we do a lot of autopsies. Several a day, every day. How long ago was the autopsy, did you say?"

"Nineteen years," Brunelle answered. "Give or take."

"Nineteen years ago?" Kaladi whistled. He nodded to Brunelle. "Nineteen years ago I was probably about your age. Now look at me."

Brunelle forced a tight smile. He wasn't that old. Not yet anyway. And either way, he didn't want to look at Kaladi and imagine himself. Brunelle was used to death, but he didn't like thinking about mortality. He ignored the tangent. "Any chance you did the autopsy?"

"There's always a chance," Kaladi said, stopping at a door marked 'Records'. "But probably not. Like I said, we do a lot of these, and there have been a lot of us who've done them."

He pushed down on the door handle and opened the door. "But come on. Let's pull the file and see what we can find out."

It took Kaladi several minutes to find the file. There were a lot of files. And they weren't even files. They were just copies of autopsy reports, shoved into a file cabinet drawer, one after another. They weren't even alphabetical; they were arranged by 'Medical Examiner Number'—which was basically just the order in which the autopsies were done. Anderson could be followed by Zechevsky, followed by Hollister. But eventually, Kaladi found Garrabalino for Brunelle and Carlisle.

"Ah-ha, here we are," Kaladi pulled the stapled-together photocopied pages out from between whoever's corpses had been carved up before and after Jenny Garrabalino's. "Let's see what we can see."

"Speaking of what we can't see," Carlisle scanned the room, "this room looks like it has nothing but paper. Is there an evidence locker section somewhere? You know, like for actual physical items?"

"No," Kaladi answered. "We have a few small lockers down near the examination rooms, to hold personal effects while we conduct the autopsy, but we don't keep anything here. Everything goes back to the relevant police agency after the autopsy is done."

"But Burien P.D. said they didn't have any evidence," Carlisle responded.

"And I know why." Kaladi pointed to the report. "There wasn't any evidence to store."

Brunelle raised an eyebrow. "What now?"

Kaladi double-checked the report. "Nope. Nothing. The only thing that was recovered was her skeleton." He looked again at the report. "And a lot of that was missing, actually."

Brunelle looked at Carlisle, who responded with a hard eye roll.

"Nothing?" Brunelle complained.

"Nope," Kaladi confirmed. "Just most of a skeleton. By the time the remains were discovered, everything else had decomposed, even the clothing."

"So, how did you know she was shot multiple times?" Carlisle asked.

"Is that how she died?" Kaladi asked. He flipped through the report. "Oh, sure enough. Well, it's pretty obvious she died from multiple gunshot wounds. Two entrance wounds to the left side of the skull. Bullet fragments in the C-7 vertebrae. And oh! Another bullet lodged in her clavicle. Well, most of it anyway. Most of the bullet, I mean. Yeah, she was definitely shot to death."

Brunelle frowned. "Were the bullets at least recovered?"

Kaladi referred to the report again. "No, those were gone too. Only the fragments lodged in her bones, and those were too damaged to be analyzed."

"So, nothing," Carlisle concluded.

"Nothing," Kaladi confirmed.

Brunelle thought for a moment. "There must have been something else. Did you do the autopsy? Maybe there's something you remember, something unusual or noteworthy."

"If it was noteworthy," Carlisle observed, "it would be noted in the report."

Kaladi agreed with a nod. "And anyway, I didn't do the autopsy. It was Jack McNamara."

"Okay, so let's talk with him," Brunelle suggested.

But Kaladi shook his head. "Oh, no. He was here when I started. This was probably one of the last cases he worked on.

He retired shortly after this and passed away soon after. He's been dead at least fifteen years."

Brunelle frowned. "Oh, sorry. I didn't know."

"No need to be sorry." Kaladi grinned. "We all die, Mr. Brunelle. The only mystery is when. And by whose hand."

CHAPTER 14

So it went, case after case, each a decade or more old, each dependent on the collection and preservation protocols in use at the time, by officers unaware what the future of forensics and murder would hold. There was also human error. In one case, there had been clothing and other evidence, but the collecting officer put everything in one bag, probably with the intent of separating it out afterward but forgetting to do so. The result was a cross-contaminated pile of moldy uselessness. Another case's evidence had gotten lost when the department moved into a new headquarters with a brand new property room. In yet another case, there had been a power outage years before that shut down the refrigeration system. The evidence in several cases, including the one Brunelle cared about, had been spoiled and destroyed.

They were halfway through Duncan's thirty-day deadline and no closer to pinning any of the murders on Kincaid.

"So, what are you going to do?" Emory asked her boyfriend after lunch a day later. They were walking back to

Brunelle's office following a quick bite at the teriyaki place around the corner.

Brunelle shrugged. "I don't know. Keep plugging away, I guess. It's all we can do. But we better hit something good soon. If we can find a case with some testable evidence, we still have to send it the crime lab and get them to drop everything to get us the results back before Duncan's deadline expires. Every day that passes makes it that much harder."

They passed through the metal detectors in the lobby of the courthouse and joined the other workers waiting for an elevator after lunch.

"Maybe Duncan is right," Emory broached. "Maybe these cases can't get solved without Kincaid's help."

Brunelle shook his head. "They definitely can't get solved without Kincaid's help," he agreed. "At least the ones we've looked at so far. But Duncan's not right. Kincaid deserves to die in prison. Anything less and we've failed all the people he did this to, whether we can prove it was him or not."

An elevator arrived and Brunelle and Emory squeezed inside. They paused their conversation on the ride up. Normal people don't want to hear about forensic analysis of murder victim remains, especially not right after lunch. They waited for their floor, then picked up the conversation again.

"Well, try to look on the bright side," Emory suggested. "You've eliminated half of the cases. There's bound to be something better in the ones left. They're more recent, right? So, better evidence preservation and collection probably."

"Maybe." Brunelle wasn't convinced. He pulled open the door to the lobby of his office. Time to say goodbye and get back to work.

"Sure," Emory soothed. "It's got to get better."

Brunelle frowned. "It could hardly get worse."

"Mr. Brunelle?" the receptionist interrupted. He was holding up a manila envelope. "A legal messenger dropped this off while you were out."

"What is it?" Emory asked, even as Brunelle took the envelope and pulled out the document inside.

"It got worse," Brunelle answered. "Edwards just filed a motion to dismiss for insufficient evidence."

CHAPTER 15

The main war room was still at Seattle P.D. H.Q., but Brunelle had recreated the whiteboard on a wall of his office. Smaller photos, but the same map, and just as unsolved as the day they first met with all the detectives.

"We're missing something," Brunelle mused, hand to his chin as he stood before the display.

"Yeah," Carlisle agreed from her chair at Brunelle's desk. "Some evidence. Of anything. By anyone. We can't prove anybody committed those murders, let alone Kincaid. No wonder they were unsolved."

Brunelle nodded, but kept his eyes fixed to the board. "The problem is the cases are so old," he said.

"The problem is," Carlisle offered a counterproposal, "the cops did a shitty job preserving everything. Better evidence collection, and we would've linked some of these to him already."

"They didn't know," Brunelle defended reflexively. Then he admitted, "But, yeah, you have a point."

Carlisle stood up and walked over to Brunelle. She

pointed at the photographs they had crossed out, no hope of the cases being solved. "These are a lost cause." She pointed to the remaining photographs. "And these are wishful thinking. We're in trouble."

Brunelle couldn't disagree.

"We just need to find the one case," he said, "where the cops actually preserved everything properly. Where the evidence was collected in the first place, properly stored, not lost or spoiled, and is ready to send off to the crime lab. One of these cases has to meet all of those requirements."

Carlisle nodded, but shrugged. "You'd think so, wouldn't you? Too bad you and I weren't there when the bodies were found. We could have helped direct everything with our current case in mind."

"Except our current case didn't exist when those bodies were found," Brunelle pointed out.

"Fair point," Carlisle conceded. "But there's not much to be done about it now."

Brunelle stared at the board. He was missing something. He knew it. The solution was right there, somewhere, but it was being blocked out by the glare of the failed cases.

Carlisle looked at the clock. "Well, Dave, I gotta go." She clapped him on the shoulder. "We both have other cases, and one of mine has a pretrial conference in twelve minutes. I need to head down to court."

Brunelle nodded again and gave an acknowledging grunt, but his attention was being drawn deeper into the information board in front of him.

"I'm missing something," he said aloud to himself after Carlisle had departed. "But what?"

CHAPTER 16

Brunelle worked late that night. Very late. He canceled his plans with Emory and sent Carlisle home at quitting time. He needed time to think, alone. He also needed to start working on his response to Edwards's motion to dismiss, which she had unknowingly scheduled for two days after Duncan's deadline.

The good news was that motions to dismiss criminal cases were rarely granted. It was supposed to be up to the jury to find a defendant not guilty, not the judge to short-circuit the process. Brunelle's evidence was thin, but the law was on his side. When a defendant made a motion to dismiss before the trial, the judge was supposed to assume all of the State's evidence was true and draw any and all reasonable inferences in favor of the State. The question was basically, could any jury, anywhere, ever possibly convict based on the evidence the State had, even if they probably wouldn't? Was there a chance? A judge wouldn't dismiss a case unless they were completely convinced no jury could ever possibly convict based on the State's flimsy evidence.

So, yes, the law was on his side. But the facts weren't. the judge might very well answer that question against him.

Brunelle looked away from his monitor and back at the case summary display he'd built on his far wall. The only case they'd gotten any evidence on was the latest one, where he and Chen stood over the body before anyone started collecting the evidence. Even then, the evidence was thin, but at least they'd known not to push the maggots away before the entomologist could come out—things like that to wring every last drop of evidence out of a scene. Even when the body had been out in the elements for a few weeks.

Brunelle paused. He stood up and walked over to the diagram.

Now that they knew how Kincaid had done the murders, they would be in an even better position to know what evidence to look for and make sure they collected it. What they needed was a case where the evidence hadn't been collected yet.

"A missing person's case," Brunelle realized.

And there were three to choose from. Three women who had disappeared under circumstances that strongly suggested Kincaid had murdered them. Three women whose remains had yet to be discovered. Three opportunities to do it right.

Brunelle rushed back to his desk and dialed Chen's number.

"Hello, you've reached the voicemail of Detective Larry Chen of the Seattle Police Department…"

"Damn," Brunelle hissed. Then, after the beep, "Larry, It's Dave. I have an idea. Call me as soon as you can."

Then a call to Carlisle. It didn't even ring, just straight to voicemail. Brunelle wondered whether her phone was off, or she had simply rejected his call.

He looked at the board again. He had an idea. A great

idea. A great, stupid, terrible, someone-should-talk-him-out-of-it idea. But still a great idea. And he didn't want to be talked out of it. Which is why he didn't call Emory before ripping the map off the wall and rushing out into the Seattle night.

CHAPTER 17

Stephanie Pang. Asian female, twenty-seven years old, long history of prostitution and drug charges, and last seen eight months ago, walking the streets on State Route 99 where White Center, Burien, and Tukwila all came together. Missing from one city and dumped in another, Brunelle suspected. Three agencies, not talking to each other—at least not until Brunelle called them all into a room together. It made for the perfect scenario for a missing woman to stay missing.

Brunelle drove through the rain, southbound on State Route 99. He had a hunch. A deduction really. He wasn't fond of hunches. He wasn't prone to them, not successful ones anyway, so he tried to stick to evidence based decision making. But sometimes several apparently disconnected facts could combine into a conclusion that really wasn't much more than a hunch. But whatever he labeled it, it was leading him back to PetMax. Back to where Ashleigh Engel's body had been found.

Accidentally. By a dog.

Brunelle realized what was missing. There were two things, actually. The women who hadn't been found were missing. But so was the chart Emory had crafted during their meeting. He had duplicated the photos and the map in his office, but not the chart, and when he remembered the chart, he knew where to look for Stephanie Pang.

Kincaid had gotten away with a lot of murders, even by his own account. He might still get away with the one he was charged with if Brunelle didn't shore up the case. But Kincaid didn't do that by being stupid. He was like anyone else who was good at his craft. He learned, he refined, and he improved. He'd just been unlucky that a Doberman dug under the fence before Ashleigh Engel was just a pile of scentless bones like Jenny Garrabalino and a few others. The only mistake Kincaid had made was leaving her body too close to a still occupied business. Otherwise, it was the perfect dump site.

Which meant, maybe, just maybe, he'd used it before. Part of refining a technique is sticking with what works.

Brunelle reached the PetMax warehouse and pulled off the street into the gravel in front of the building. The Doberman's junkyard was to his right, two lots to the north. But south of the PetMax warehouse was nothing but more abandoned warehouses and storefronts, all abutting some woods that bounded the back of the industrial district there. The kind of woods no one ever really went into. Perfect.

Brunelle turned south and rolled forward on the gravel, his tires crunching as he paralleled State Route 99, using the connected parking areas of the abandoned buildings as a sort of access road. He could move slowly, examining the area, without fear of another car barreling down on him. Although, as it was, there were no other cars on the road. There was no one else around at all. Again, perfect.

Brunelle's car continued its southerly crawl as he

scanned the woods between the spaced-out buildings to his left. Ashleigh Engel was dumped approximately eight months after Stephanie Pang disappeared. Engel had been found, but Pang hadn't. Kincaid wouldn't have dumped Engel there if he didn't think she wouldn't be found either. Which meant he thought it was a good hiding place. Because, Brunelle surmised, it had worked before.

"Bingo," Brunelle said to himself as he cleared another building and the next abandoned warehouse came into view. It wasn't just abandoned; it was cordoned off with portable sections of chain-link fence. The fence surrounded the building on three sides, the ends of the fence jutting into the trees on either side of the structure, plywood covering its windows and graffiti covering its walls, notwithstanding the large 'No Trespassing' signs hung every ten feet on the fencing. Third time perfect.

Perfect for Kincaid. The perfect place to dump a body.

Perfect for Brunelle. The perfect place to look for the remains of Stephanie Pang.

Chen hadn't answered any of his calls, but if Brunelle found a body, he could call 9-1-1 and wait for the responders. He could make sure any evidence was secured in a way that would bolster his case against Kincaid.

Brunelle turned away from the road and rolled to the very back of the lot, about fifteen feet from the fence. To be safe, he was going to start outside the fence, although he suspected Kincaid would have been unlikely to pass up the extra security of the fence and 'No Trespassing' signs. But still, Brunelle thought, no stone—or skull or femur—unturned.

He put the car in park, but kept the engine running and the headlights on to give himself some light in the otherwise black night. The rain was still present, but not overly so. It was Seattle. He got rained on. That was life, even when looking for death.

He stepped out and trudged into the woods directly in front of his car. The grass was tall and wet, and the leaves dripped cold raindrops down the back of his shirt. He was still in his suit, but the suit was due for the dry cleaners anyway. Still, he tried to watch his step, lest he sink too deep in the mud and ruin his shoes. Those couldn't go to the dry cleaners.

Not surprisingly, there wasn't a dead body as soon as he entered the narrow strip of trees. There was only about five feet or so before it dropped off steeply toward the river below. He wasn't going to risk sliding down into the water, and he bet Kincaid hadn't been willing to risk it either, especially with a dead body in his arms. Time wouldn't have been on his side. It was dump and run. Which was also why Brunelle didn't start even farther away from the chain-link fence.

In short order, Brunelle had reached that fence. His shoes were definitely muddy, as were the cuffs of his pants. His hands and wrists were wet from pushing aside branches. He thought it sounded like the rain might be letting up, but it was hard to tell inside the patch of trees. The fence jutted about four feet into the woods from the gravel. That gave Brunelle only a foot or so to pass around behind it and enter the grounds of whatever shuttered business was still so important to someone to bother fencing it off. He grabbed ahold of the fence to test its strength. A few stout pulls confirmed it was sturdy enough. He sidled to the end of it, then grabbed ahold and swung himself around the terminal pole. He was inside, although he began to doubt himself as he couldn't imagine Kincaid, or anyone, swinging themselves around the fence post like that while carrying a dead body.

Still, he'd come this far. He decided to make his way to the fence on the other side, and if he didn't find anything—anyone, rather—he'd call it a night. A wet, muddy night. And he'd definitely walk back around to the front of the building. Maybe the rain would wash some of the mud off his shoes.

He squelched deeper into the woods. His headlights were far behind him now, and he relied on the small flashlight he'd taken from the glove compartment. He'd used it before on a rainy night, but never to look for a dead body. *First time for everything,* he supposed.

He expected Kincaid probably wouldn't have bothered going too far past the fence. Just far enough to drop the body and get out again. Even so, Kincaid might have parked by the other end of the fence and dumped the body there, at the far end of Brunelle's trek.

Or maybe not.

The sound of a bone breaking under his muddy shoe let Brunelle know his hunch/deduction had been right.

Sticks sounded a certain way when they broke, especially wet sticks. Bones were different. They didn't get wet inside, and they splintered when they broke. A cascade of smaller breaking noises assembled into the noise Brunelle heard when he stepped on, and broke, the shin bone of Stephanie Pang.

He shined his flashlight straight down to confirm what he already knew. He carefully stepped off the bone he'd cracked and illuminated what was left of Kincaid's penultimate victim. The remains were half covered by fallen leaves and overgrown grass, but the rib cage and skull were unmistakable, even in the weak light of his portable flashlight.

They were even more unmistakable when the entire area was suddenly floodlit by several high-powered flashlights, all closing in on his position.

"Police! Put your hands on your head and get down on your knees. You're under arrest."

CHAPTER 18

Brunelle did as ordered—of course. He set the flashlight down, slowly, then put his hands on his head and lowered himself even more slowly into a kneeling position. A silhouetted police officer grabbed one of his wrists and forced him onto his stomach. So much for the suit. He had rain and mud up to his chin as the officer pulled him to his feet, his hands securely cuffed behind his back.

Having successfully neutralized his suspect, the handcuffing officer took a moment to apprise his catch, even as his partner continued past them to see what Brunelle had been looking at. That wasn't going to help matters, Brunelle knew.

"You don't look like a trespasser," the arresting officer commented.

"I'm not," Brunelle answered. Then he thought about it a little more. It wasn't like those 'No Trespassing' signs made an exception for homicide prosecutors. "I mean, I guess maybe I am. But that's not why I'm here."

"Oh, shit! Bill!" the other officer called out to his partner.

Brunelle nodded. "That's why I'm here."

"What is it?" Handcuffer asked.

"It's a dead body," the other officer announced. "We caught ourselves a murderer."

Brunelle sighed. Maybe he should have called Emory after all.

It was a bit of a blur in the moments after that. Suit or no suit, he was suddenly a murder suspect. The kid gloves were off. And he was back on the ground, a knee between his shoulders.

"What the hell are you doing out here, mister?" the first officer demanded. He had taken two steps back and assumed a ready stance, his gun drawn and pointed at Brunelle's head.

"You might want to read me my rights first, guys," Brunelle said, his cheek against the wet gravel. "I'm pretty sure my freedom is restricted to the degree associated with formal arrest, which is the legal standard, after all."

The officers traded looks.

"Are you a lawyer or something?" the one with his knee in Brunelle's back asked, again without Mirandizing him.

"Or something," Brunelle answered. "I'm a prosecutor. A homicide prosecutor, actually. That's why I'm out here. I'm investigating a missing persons case that just turned into a murder case."

"You're investigating?" the back officer questioned.

"You're not a cop," the gun officer noted.

"I'm prosecuting a case where a body was found just up the road," Brunelle tried to explain. "I was driving by when I thought maybe there might be another body a little farther down."

"That seems awfully suspicious," Back Officer said. "You just happened to know where a body was buried?"

"It's not buried," Brunelle pointed out. "It was just dumped here, like eight months ago."

"And how would you know when she was dumped?"

"Unless you're the one who dumped her?"

Brunelle let out a deep sigh. "You know how I can ask to call a lawyer at any time? I think I'd like to call a detective. Maybe he'll pick up finally."

* * *

In the event, Chen did not pick up. Or rather, the officers did not bother calling him. They pulled Brunelle to his feet, then shoved him in the back of one of their two patrol cars. Brunelle had to sit there, wet and dirty, and just wait while the officers secured the scene, which he noted with some dismay, included his car. They turned it off, locked it, and kept the keys for safekeeping. He could only hope they'd leave the body alone until whatever detective was on call that night arrived at the scene. If it was Chen, he'd know to preserve everything with Kincaid in mind. But if it was any of the other detectives at Seattle P.D., it was a crapshoot whether they knew enough about Chen's case to recognize they were related. Just like Kincaid had always banked on.

When Officer Handcuffer finally climbed into the driver's seat of the patrol vehicle twenty minutes later, Brunelle immediately implored him to protect the evidence.

"You have to seal off the scene," he said. "This may be our only chance to link another case to the man who murdered the other woman found up the road."

"And that person isn't you?" The officer seemed incredulous. "I'm pretty sure I don't take orders from murder suspects."

"I'm not a murder suspect," Brunelle insisted. "I'm a

murder prosecutor."

"You're under arrest for trespassing is what you are," the officer responded, starting the engine. "You better hope it doesn't get worse."

CHAPTER 19

An arrestee didn't actually get one phone call as soon as they reached the station. That would be a stupid rule. Suspects could call accomplices to destroy evidence or worse. No, an arrestee would only have access to a phone once they were booked into the jail, just like any other inmate. In the meantime, if they were arrested for murder, they would be put in an interrogation room to await the arrival of a detective. Brunelle had been doing homicides long enough, he knew most of the detectives who might be coming in to talk to him, even if it wasn't Chen. He just had to be patient. It was all a big misunderstanding. The important thing was, they had found another body, and Brunelle had no doubt Kincaid was responsible for Stephanie Pang's murder too.

When the door to the interrogation room finally slammed open and Brunelle looked up at the person who entered the room, his heart sank. He had no idea who she was.

She was in her late 40s, Brunelle guessed, with red hair pulled back into a thick ponytail. No makeup and a serious expression on her face, jeans and a leather jacket adorning her solid frame. The fact that she was a cop was only discernable from the badge clipped to her hip. There was a gun on the other hip.

"I'm Detective Sally Winthrop," the woman announced. "I'd like to ask you a few questions about your activities tonight, Mr. uh, Brunelle, is it?"

"Yes, David Brunelle," he confirmed. "I'm a prosecutor with the King County Prosecuting Attorney's Office. If you could just get ahold of Detective Larry Chen—"

"Now, hold on just a second, sir," Winthrop raised a palm at him. "We haven't verified your identity yet. I'm not calling anyone until I figure out exactly what you were doing out in the middle of the night with the body of a dead hooker we've been trying to find for over six months."

"Eight months," Brunelle clarified.

"Now, see," Winthrop pointed at Brunelle, "when you do that, it makes me think maybe you know a little too much about this case. Since you apparently know when the victim died, it makes me think maybe you were there when it happened."

Brunelle just stared at Winthrop for several seconds. He couldn't believe what was happening. And while they were wasting time in there, God only knew whether the forensics team out at Stephanie Pang's body was doing what needed to be done to catch Kincaid.

"I did not kill Stephanie Pang," Brunelle said. "Now, if you'll just listen to me for a—"

"You know her name?" Winthrop clicked her tongue at him. "Well, now I'm sure you were involved. How'd you know her? Were you one of her regulars? Is that what happened? You got a little jealous? Offered to be her sugar daddy? Take her away from all this? But then she said no. You were just another john to her. There was never any emotion on her end. She just faked it to keep you coming back. And you couldn't handle that, could you? And that's why you snapped? Isn't it, Brunelle?" Winthrop slammed a fist down on the table in front of him. "That's why you killed her! Admit it!"

Brunelle pushed back in his chair, away from any further fists. His hands were still cuffed behind his back. It never should have gone this far, so he had no confidence in where it would go next. They still hadn't read him his *Miranda* rights.

"I, uh I think I better talk to..." Brunelle started, but he trailed off. If he asked for a lawyer, the interview would be over—probably—and he would just get booked. It would be hours before he could get to a phone to call Chen to preserve the crime scene, and Carlisle to vouch for him, and Emory to bail him out.

"I, uh, I, uh, I think, uh..." Winthrop mocked him. "You think a jury is going to believe that pack of lies?"

Brunelle cocked his head at her. "I didn't even say anything."

"Damn right you didn't," Winthrop shot back. "Because that's what guilty people do. Stumble and stammer and then they confess. So, why don't we just skip to the good part? Go ahead and confess, Brunelle. Come on, confess."

"But I didn't do anything," Brunelle protested.

"You trespassed," Winthrop pointed out.

Brunelle sighed. "Yes, that's true. I trespassed."

"And you went out to a crime scene without any police backup," Winthrop continued.

Brunelle thought for a moment. "Um, that's true, I guess, although that's not a crime—"

"And worst of all," Winthrop leaned onto the table and shoved a finger in his face, "you didn't even call your girlfriend before you went out and trespassed and found a dead body and got yourself arrested, now did you?"

Brunelle blinked at Winthrop. Then he looked up at the observation camera in the corner of the ceiling. "Are you fucking kidding me?" he called out.

Winthrop broke up laughing. A few moments later, the door opened again and in came Chen and Emory, both laughing at least as hard as Winthrop.

Brunelle wasn't laughing.

"Oh my God, Dave," Emory gasped. "You should have seen your face when Linda walked in and you didn't know who she was. I thought you were gonna piss your pants."

"Linda Winthrop," Winthrop introduced herself. "Bellevue P.D."

"And fuck you too," Brunelle snapped back. "Can someone get these handcuffs off me, please?"

Emory held up the key but hesitated. "You have to promise not to be mad."

"I have to promise not to be mad before you unhandcuff me?" Brunelle questioned. "That's kind of making me even more angry."

"Uh-oh," Chen put in. "You wouldn't like him when he's angry."

Brunelle let out another sigh and shrugged. "Fine. Whatever. I'm not mad. But I am worried. Is the crime scene okay? Did those two officers ruin it before you got called in?"

"Well, some idiot stepped on the skeleton and broke one of the bones, but otherwise everything looks fine," Chen answered. "I got the callout and when the patrol guy told me they'd arrested an old guy in a suit, I knew exactly what had happened."

"I'm not that old," Brunelle insisted as Emory unlocked his handcuffs. "And in my defense, it was dark out. I didn't see the skeleton until I was on top of it. Literally."

Brunelle rubbed his wrists and stood up, his back cracking as he did so.

"Are you okay?" Emory asked. "You're not mad, are you? We were just having some fun with you. You really should have called me."

"You would have talked me out of it," Brunelle said.

"I would have gone with you, you idiot," Emory shoved him.

"You did it, Dave," Chen interjected. "You found another of Kincaid's victims. This is the breakthrough we needed."

Brunelle shook his head. "Not yet it isn't. Proximity in time and place isn't going to be enough. We're going to need something solid connecting Kincaid to that crime scene, or this is all for nothing."

CHAPTER 20

Days passed with no news. There hadn't been any obvious smoking gun at the Pang crime scene. No business card with Kincaid's name on it hidden under the victim's body. No clutch of Kincaid's hair in her hand. Just another skeleton, completely decomposed, with a bullet hole in the left side of her skull. But there was no bullet found inside her skull. It had likely fallen out after all the soft tissue rotted away, maybe when the body was disturbed by animals or a particularly hard rainstorm.

Day 30 of Duncan's deadline arrived with no forensic way of connecting the crimes. At 4:45 p.m., Carlisle and Brunelle were sitting in Brunelle's office, wishing against the inevitable.

Brunelle pushed himself up out of his chair. "I better go tell Matt we couldn't do it."

But Carlisle grabbed his arm. "No, don't. Today is Day Thirty, but the day isn't over yet."

Brunelle laughed. "It's the end of the workday. Nothing is going to change overnight. I'm done getting arrested at crime scenes late at night."

"Just wait," Carlisle repeated. She let go of his arm. "Tell him tomorrow morning. Something might come up. It has to."

"It might," Brunelle agreed, "but it doesn't have to."

"Do you know the story of the sultan's horse?" Carlisle asked suddenly.

Brunelle's eyebrows raised. "Uh, no. I don't think I do. Is this a real story?"

"It's a parable," Carlisle answered.

"Great." Brunelle rolled his eyes.

"No, hear me out," Carlisle said. "There once was this sultan who owned a prize horse. He had a jester, too, and one day the jester made the wrong joke and offended the sultan. The sultan sentenced him to death, but the jester made an eloquent plea for his life. He said, 'Sultan, give me a year, and I will teach your prize horse to talk. You will be the most famous and celebrated sultan in the world with your amazing talking horse.' The sultan thought about it for a while and then agreed. 'I will give you one year to teach my horse to talk,' he announced. 'But if you fail, you will be executed.' The sultan left and a friend of the jester came up to him and said, 'You've just delayed the inevitable.' But the jester shrugged. 'A lot can happen in a year,' he said. 'The sultan might die. I might die. Or... the horse might talk'."

When she'd finished, Brunelle stared at her for a moment. "Is that it?"

"Yes," Carlisle said. "That's it."

Brunelle narrowed his eyes. "And the moral of the story is...?"

"Don't ever give up," Carlisle answered. "There's still time. You don't know what might happen between now and tomorrow morning."

"But there's no horse in this case," Brunelle teased.

"Really, Dave?" Carlisle crossed her arms. "I'm being serious here."

"You just told me a story about a talking horse," Brunelle pointed out, "but fine. I bet Matt is waiting for me to come see him right at five, so I'll head out the back stairs now. If he comes looking for me, play dumb."

"That's not a natural thing for me, you know," Carlisle quipped.

"I do know," Brunelle answered. "I just don't think it's going to matter."

CHAPTER 21

Nothing changed overnight. The horse didn't talk. And the sultan hadn't died either. The only thing that was dead was their case against Kincaid. Ten years for twenty-plus murders. That wasn't justice. But it was the agreement he'd made with Duncan.

Brunelle arrived at work and went directly to Duncan's office.

"Hey, Matt, you got a minute?" Brunelle said as he knocked on the doorframe to Duncan's office. His office door was always open, literally and metaphorically. "I wanted to update you on the Kincaid case."

"Sure, Dave." Duncan motioned for Brunelle to come in and sit down. "I was expecting you to stop by. Actually, I kinda thought you'd stop by at the end of the day yesterday."

Brunelle grimaced. "Yeah, me too. But I had to see a man about a horse."

Duncan cocked his head. "What?"

"Nothing." Brunelle waved it away. "Never mind. The important thing is," a heavy sigh, "we weren't able to connect any of those other cases to Kincaid. You gave me thirty days to do it, and the thirty days is up. So, we do it your way."

Duncan didn't smile. In fact, he frowned a bit. "You know this isn't how I wanted it to go. I wanted you to connect him up to more murders. I wanted you to take him down. But if we can't do that, Dave, we have to take this offer. We play the cards we're dealt."

"Yeah, I'm kind of done with metaphors right now," Brunelle said. "It's a murder case. It's thin. I could lose. He'll plead guilty for a reduced sentence. Bonus: we close a bunch of cold cases that I can tell you now with absolute certainty were never going to be solved. Not with what evidence is left."

Duncan stood up and extended a hand. "Thanks for understanding, Dave. Let me know what his lawyer says."

"She's going to say, 'Told you so'," Brunelle guessed even as he shook his boss's hand. "Or some variation on that theme. But that's okay. I'll get her next time."

"There's always a next time, isn't there?" Duncan chuckled.

"Yes, sir," Brunelle agreed. "As long as there are psychos like Michael James Kincaid."

It was a slow, painful walk back to Brunelle's office. A slow, painful walk across the office to his desk. A slow, painful motion to pick up the telephone. He started dialing Edwards's number, slowly. Painfully.

"Hang up!" Carlisle shouted from the doorway. She had a sheet of paper in her hand.

Brunelle was only too happy to abort that particular phone call. "What is it?" He let himself hope maybe the bullets matched after all. But it was even better.

"Remember that trace amount of DNA in Kincaid's

trunk?" Carlisle asked. "The ones that weren't Ashleigh Engel?"

"No way." Brunelle knew what she was going to say. He just couldn't believe it.

"Yup." Carlisle beamed. "It was Stephanie Pang."

The horse talked after all. And it told Duncan, 'No.'

CHAPTER 22

Edwards's motion to dismiss was scheduled for argument before Judge Sarah Nunberg, another of the fifty or so judges on the King County Superior Court. She'd been appointed by the governor, then reelected twice, the second time unopposed. She had a reputation for being prepared but also a little rude, making sure the attorneys who appeared before her knew who was really in charge. Of course, that was because judges hated to admit they weren't really in charge. They were referees. They got to make the calls, but it was the coaches and players who were really in charge of the game. So, they could have drawn a better judge, but they could have drawn worse. But Brunelle wasn't worried. He was pretty sure he knew they weren't going to need a referee after all.

"Morning, Jess," he said as he set his materials down on the prosecution table. Carlisle had walked in with him, but she wasn't interested in greeting her opponents. "Morning, Pete."

"Good morning, Mr. Brunelle," Saxby responded eagerly. Then he remembered. "I mean, Dave."

Brunelle went ahead and smiled a bit. He couldn't

decide if Saxby's baby lawyer act was endearing or annoying. Probably both.

"Last chance, Dave," Edwards turned from her own counsel table and put her fists on her hips. "Guilty plea to murder and a whole lot of unsolved cases suddenly solved. Or Judge Nunberg takes the bench, and your case gets dismissed."

"I think there's a third option," Brunelle answered. He pulled some documents from his file. "These are for you."

Edwards accepted the paperwork reluctantly. "What are these? It's too late to supplement your briefing now. The hearing is about to start."

"It's not briefing, Jess," Brunelle answered. "The top document is a copy of the police reports for a body recovered approximately a half mile south of where your client dumped Ashleigh Engel. Under that is a copy of the crime lab report establishing that the DNA of this new victim was present in the trunk of your client's car. And at the very bottom is your copy of the new criminal complaint charging your client with a second count of murder in the first degree."

Edwards stared at the documents for a few seconds, then up again at Brunelle. "You've been busy."

"So have you," Brunelle responded with a wave around the courtroom. "I had to do something."

The secure side door to the courtroom opened with a clank and in walked Kincaid, handcuffed and flanked by two corrections officers.

"You're going to lose your motion now, Jess," Brunelle put in before Edwards turned around to greet and check in with her client.

Edwards just frowned, then gestured to the bailiff. "I'm going to need a few minutes to speak with my client before the judge comes out, please."

The bailiff agreed and picked up the phone, presumably to tell the judge to wait before taking the bench.

"I generally avoid looking at defendants," Carlisle said to Brunelle in a lowered voice, "but I'd love to see his face when Jessica tells him we've pinned another murder on him."

Brunelle couldn't help but turn to steal a glance over his shoulder, but Saxby's body was effectively blocking Kincaid from their view. For her part, Edwards appeared to be doing all of the talking, pointing to the documents Brunelle had just given her while doing so. They knew roughly what she was telling him.

After a few minutes, Edwards patted Kincaid on the shoulder, then stood up again and walked back over to Brunelle and Carlisle. Saxby scrambled to follow suit.

She held up the new criminal complaint. "Have you filed this yet?"

Brunelle shook his head. "No, not yet."

"Good," Edwards exhaled. "Don't."

"Excuse me?" Carlisle put in. "We don't work for you."

"Don't file it *yet*," Edwards clarified. "Let me talk with my guy. Maybe we can still work out a deal."

"Strike the motion to dismiss then," Brunelle countered.

"No, concede it," Carlisle said. "If it's stricken, she can renote it. Concede we have enough evidence to go to a jury and we'll consider holding off filing the new murder charge. For now."

Edwards stared at Carlisle for a moment, then looked back to Brunelle. "Okay, so this is your case, right, Dave? You make the call. You know I'm not conceding anything in the heat of the moment. Let's just call a time out and assess where we are. I'll strike—not concede—my motion. You hold off filing the new charge for a day or two. Let me talk with my guy."

"Why?" Carlisle demanded. "What good will that do?"

Edwards still directed her response to Brunelle. "This guy wants to make a deal. Maybe I can push him up to something you can accept."

"Doubtful," Carlisle sneered.

"But not impossible," Brunelle conceded. "One day. We hold off filing the new charge until the end of business tomorrow. You strike today's hearing. You talk to your guy, then you talk to me."

"Us," Carlisle corrected.

"Right," Brunelle agreed. He pointed to both Edwards and Saxby. "You two talk to us two."

"And then we'll file the new charge," Carlisle said.

Brunelle stifled a sigh. The bravado wasn't particularly helpful just then.

Edwards pointed at Brunelle, then at herself. "Dave? You and me? We understand each other, right?"

Brunelle nodded. "Right, Jess. One day. Talk fast."

Edwards walked over to the bailiff, and they could overhear her saying the defense was striking the hearing, for now. No need for the judge to come out. She told the same thing to the corrections officers and authorized them to return Kincaid to his cell. Then she practically grabbed Saxby by the lapels and pulled him to the exit with her. In a few minutes, the only people left in the courtroom were Brunelle and Carlisle.

"We should have just done the hearing," Carlisle complained. "We would have won, and then we'd have even more leverage over her."

Brunelle wasn't so sure. "We would have won," he

agreed, "but our leverage is the same. She knows no judge is going to throw out two murder cases against the same defendant. She won't renote the motion. We won, for all intents and purposes."

"And what about this new offer she's going to make?" Carlisle worried. "Duncan almost made us take the last one."

"That's true." Brunelle nodded. "But he didn't. And I bet we can talk him out of it again, no matter what the offer is."

"Yeah…" Carlisle crossed her arms and nodded at length. "I bet you're wrong."

CHAPTER 23

The room was dim. One of the two banks of fluorescent lights was out, and there were no windows. They decided not to smash into a two-person attorney-client meeting room again. Instead, they commandeered the jail library, housed in an interior room on the third floor. It was a lot bigger, but also filled with things a desperate inmate facing life in prison might use to assault someone with. It had happened before.

So, Kincaid sat at the far end of one of the tables, his hands cuffed both behind his back and also through the opening in the back of the chair. If he tried to stand up, he'd have his hands behind him, and would be pulling his chair along for the ride. That would make him slow enough for Chen or the corrections officers guarding the door to drop him before anyone could be hurt.

But Kincaid didn't seem like he wanted a fight. He wanted a talk.

Carlisle wanted a fight. "Can we get started already?" she complained. "I've got other plans tonight."

"Is that right?" Kincaid asked with a leer.

She pointed at Kincaid. "You, shut the fuck up."

"You're here to talk to him," Edwards pointed out. "Like, that's the entire point."

"We're here for him to beg for his miserable life," Carlisle responded directly to Edwards. "Anything else is out of bounds. Period."

"My partner has a point," Brunelle put in. "Let's cut to the chase. You know we can link you to another murder, so you want to make a new offer. Fine. Spit it out."

"You can *try* to link him to another murder," Edwards couldn't help but say.

"I don't really have the patience for this, Jess," Brunelle responded. "You were the one who asked us to hold off charging. You were the one who said your guy wanted to talk." He looked at Kincaid. "So, talk."

"I would be happy to," Kincaid replied. "I agree with both you and my own attorney. You say you can link me to another murder; she says you can try. Those are both true."

"What do you want, you psychopath?" Carlisle butted in. She had even less patience than Brunelle.

Meanwhile, Chen stood against the wall at the far end of the room, arms crossed, looking almost bored. Saxby sat next to Edwards, looking definitely scared.

Kincaid grinned at Carlisle, but it was cold. He held it a beat too long, then directed his answer Brunelle. "I will agree to fifteen years instead of ten, and I will still tell you where all the other bodies are."

"We know where the other bodies are, Kincaid," Brunelle answered. "And it's only a matter of time until we connect even more of them to you. The mandatory minimum for Murder One is twenty years, so we'd still have to amend down to Murder Two to get to fifteen years. If we weren't willing to amend down before, what makes you think we'd be willing to do it now, after we've connected you to another murder?"

"Because you've had a month and you only connected me to one other case," Kincaid answered evenly. "And even that connection is attenuated."

"Not when I put the two cases together," Brunelle responded.

"*If*," Edwards corrected. "If you put them together. You have to get the Court's permission for a joint trial. And I'll have my motion to sever for separate trials ready at the arraignment."

"The evidence is clearly cross-admissible, Jess," Brunelle responded. "I would call all the same witnesses in separate trials, and there's a mountain of case law that says joint trials are favored."

"Maybe, for judicial economy," Edwards retorted, "but not just outcomes. You just want the jury to hear he killed two people, so they won't even listen to how thin the evidence is."

"The DNA from one murder being in his car after the other murder is relevant, Jess," Brunelle said. "You can't deny that."

"It may be relevant under ER 401," Edwards admitted, "but relevant evidence can still be excluded under ER 403 if it's unduly prejudicial or if it's likely to confuse the jury."

"If anything," Brunelle replied, "it will make everything crystal clear for the jury."

"May I interrupt?" Kincaid interrupted.

Brunelle and Edwards both looked at him.

"I don't think we're here to argue the evidence rules or the dangers of a joint trial," Kincaid said. "I think we're here to avoid all of that."

Carlisle pushed her chair back and stood up. "I'm ready to avoid all of this. Fifteen years isn't enough. End of negotiations." She looked to Brunelle. "Can we go now?"

"Why don't you go, but Mr. Brunelle stay?" Kincaid suggested. "In fact, why doesn't everyone except Mr. Brunelle leave? I think we may have a more productive conversation if there were less people involved."

"Well, I'm staying, obviously," Edwards said.

"No, I don't think that's a good idea," Kincaid replied. "It will be more productive if it can be just one-on-one."

"I'm ethically prohibited from speaking directly to someone who's represented by an attorney," Brunelle pointed out.

"Even if the person doesn't object?" Kincaid asked.

"Even then," Brunelle answered. "It's the other lawyer's right to be present, not the person's."

"So, Ms. Edwards could agree to it, and you wouldn't be violating any ethical rules?" Kincaid probed.

"This is fucking ridiculous!" Carlisle threw her hands over her head.

"So, that's a yes, I take it?" Kincaid said.

Brunelle cocked his head at Edwards. Edwards rolled her eyes and sighed. "Yes. I can agree to it," she admitted. "But it's a terrible idea."

"Why?" Kincaid said. "I think it's the safest way for me to talk to the prosecutor. You said everything I say as part of plea negotiations is inadmissible under those evidence rules, And to make it even safer for me, there would be no other witnesses, so he couldn't prove anything I said anyway, unless he was going to call himself as a witness which I suspect isn't usually permitted." He pointed at Chen, still cross-armed at the end of the table. "As it stands now, he could put the Detective on the stand to tell the jury everything I'm saying, if he could convince the judge not to honor that particular evidence rule about plea negotiations. Everything you say can and will be used against you, am I right?"

Brunelle didn't say anything for several moments.

So, Carlisle did. "You're not seriously considering this, are you?"

Brunelle finally nodded. "Yeah, okay. Everybody out."

"Seriously?" Carlisle gasped.

"Dave, I'm not sure this is a good idea," Edwards cautioned.

But Brunelle ignored them and looked over to Chen, who returned the glance with a silent nod. He stood up and crossed the room to Kincaid. Then he grabbed the back of Kincaid's chair and yanked him backwards against the cinder block wall. He grabbed the table, turned it sideways, and pushed it all the way up against Kincaid's stomach. Between that and his hands still cuffed behind his back, Kincaid wasn't going to do anything more than talk.

"I'll be right outside," Chen said, then went exactly there.

"Dave? Really?" Carlisle entreated.

"Really," Brunelle answered. "This won't take long. Will it, Kincaid?"

"Call me Michael," Kincaid replied. "And no, not long at all, I imagine."

Edwards frowned. Saxby, forced out of his seat by Chen's furniture rearranging, was standing nervously behind her. "Are you sure about this, Dave?" Edwards asked.

"Yeah, I'm sure." He looked again at Kincaid. "I can take

five minutes out of my life if it gets us closer to justice."

"Justice is giving *me* five minutes alone with him," Carlisle growled.

Kincaid started to say something back, but Edwards cut him off. "No. You want your little talk with the prosecutor, then you shut up. Do you hear me?"

Kincaid nodded. "Yes, ma'am." He was even smarmy to his own attorney.

"Five minutes," Carlisle said to Brunelle.

But Brunelle shrugged. "It will take as long as it takes. But like I said, I think I'll be out pretty quick. Enjoy the break."

Carlisle scowled at him, clearly wanting to say more, but she just let out a loud huff and stormed outside to join Chen.

"I hope you know what you're doing," Edwards cautioned Brunelle. Then she motioned to Saxby. "Come on, Pete. Let's wait outside while our client talks alone with the prosecutor. God, there's a sentence I never thought I'd say."

"First time for everything," Brunelle said after her as she stepped out into the hallway and closed the door behind her.

"And a next time for everything," Kincaid added from his penned in position across the room from Brunelle. "You know that, don't you? That's why you don't want to give me a deal."

"I don't want to give you a deal," Brunelle answered, "because you're a psychopathic murderer who deserves to die in prison."

But Kincaid shook his head. "No, that's not it. Oh, that may be part of it, but you cut deals all the time for people who deserve more punishment. That's what plea bargaining is, right? And most criminal cases resolve by way of plea bargain. Even murder cases. If I'd just killed one person, another man in a bar parking lot, both of us drunk, arguing over a girl, you would already have offered me that Murder Two."

"I would have offered the Murder Two because it was a one-off," Brunelle returned. "An alcohol driven mistake, unlikely ever to be repeated, especially after ten years in prison. But you…"

"I'm going to do it again," Kincaid finished for him.

"Yes," Brunelle confirmed. "And I can't let that happen."

"I'm not sure you can stop it, Prosecutor," Kincaid said. "Your cases against me are razor thin. Even worse if Ms. Edwards succeeds in keeping them separate for trial. What will you do if I'm acquitted? You won't harm me. That's not who you are. You'll just watch while I walk out of the front door of the jail. And you know exactly what I'm going to do."

"We know who you are now," Brunelle ventured. "You can't just get away with it anymore."

"You aren't going to put me under constant surveillance," Kincaid scoffed. "You don't have the manpower for that. And I can always move away. Another county, another state. Somewhere they don't know me. It doesn't matter where. There will always be women like Ashleigh Engel and Stephanie Pang."

Brunelle's jaw clenched at the sound of their names in Kincaid's mouth.

"But if you accept my offer," Kincaid went on, "that's fifteen years where women like that will be safe. I'd say you'd have fifteen years to tie another case to me, but part of the deal is you won't charge me for any of the murders I tell you about. But who knows? Maybe I'll die in prison. Maybe fifteen years in prison, and I won't even want to do it again. Although, if I'm completely honest, I doubt that. Still, it's a possibility. But there's no possibility of that if I walk out of here in a month because you couldn't quite prove your cases beyond a reasonable doubt."

Brunelle had to admit, Kincaid had a point. Fifteen years with him in prison was fifteen years where women like Ashleigh Engel and Stephanie Pang would be safe. Well, safer.

"So, what do you say, Prosecutor?" Kincaid looked up from where he was handcuffed to and barricaded behind jail furniture. Somehow, he still looked like he thought he was in charge.

Brunelle thought for a few more moments. Duncan would support the decision. Chen would understand it. Carlisle would get over it. And it wasn't like Ashleigh or Stephanie had any friends or family he would have to justify it to. Not any that cared, apparently.

"What do you say?" Kincaid repeated.

"I say," Brunelle sighed and extended a hand, as if to shake—then turned it over and extended his middle finger, "fuck you."

CHAPTER 24

"What did Duncan say," Carlisle asked as they walked to the courtroom for the arraignment on the new murder charge, "when you told him about Kincaid's new offer?"

"Um, what?" Brunelle asked after a moment.

"What did Duncan say?" Carlisle repeated. "Was he tempted to take it, or did this second case carry the day again?"

"Yeah, um, the thing is," Brunelle reached out and opened the courtroom door, "I didn't actually tell him about it."

Carlisle stopped, the chatter from inside the arraignment courtroom spilling into the hallway through the door held ajar by her partner. "You didn't tell him?"

"I didn't want to bother him?" Brunelle half-asked. "Anyway, I'm pretty sure I know what his answer would have been."

Carlisle grinned. "And that's why you didn't tell him."

Brunelle winked at her. "Bingo."

"You better hope he doesn't find out," Carlisle cautioned.

"I'm just going to hope we win the case," Brunelle

countered. "Then it won't matter what the offer might have been."

Carlisle smiled more broadly as she walked past him into the busy courtroom. "I endorse that plan."

Jessica Edwards, on the other hand, did not. She had not been pleased when her client sent her out of the room to talk with Brunelle. She was even less pleased when Brunelle emerged without a deal. Now she was going to have to defend two murder cases instead of just one.

"Where do you want to stand for the arraignment, Dave?" she snarked. "With Carlisle or with my client? He's still my client, right?"

"He is definitely still your client," Brunelle returned. "I don't think our conversation ended well. Not for him anyway." He pulled out the charging documents for the murder of Stephanie Pang. "Ready?"

Edwards sneered at him. "Oh, I'm ready, Dave."

So was the judge, who emerged from his chambers to the call of his bailiff. "All rise! The King County Superior Court is now in session, The Honorable Edward Carpenter presiding."

Judge Carpenter was still stuck in the criminal arraignment court. That was good news. At least he'd remember Kincaid. It hadn't been that long since the first arraignment.

"Are there any matters ready?" the judge inquired as he sat down above the courtroom.

Brunelle stepped forward. "The parties are ready on the matter of *The State of Washington versus Michael James Kincaid*," he said. "Again."

Edwards rolled her eyes at Brunelle's extra word. But Judge Carpenter raised his eyebrows at it, even as Edwards signaled to the guards to bring in her client.

"Again?" the judge asked.

"Anew," Brunelle said as he handed copies of the charging documents to the bailiff.

Judge Carpenter accepted the documents from his bailiff and perused them as Kincaid was led into the courtroom to stand next to Edwards..

"This matter comes on for arraignment," Brunelle announced, "on one count of murder in the first degree."

He was doing this arraignment, not Carlisle. Similarly, Saxby was standing in the back of the courtroom, far away from the action.

Judge Carpenter looked confused. "Are you amending the charges? I thought it was already murder in the first degree? We did this already, right?"

"Same charge," Brunelle explained. "Different victim."

Carpenter's eyebrows shot up even higher than before. "He's murdered someone since the arraignment? In the jail? I would have expected to have heard about that."

"No, Your Honor, not in the jail," Brunelle answered. "This actually predates the other case. It's a separate victim from a separate incident. The only thing the same is the crime charged. And the defendant."

Judge Carpenter studied the charging document. "Stephanie Pang," he read the victim's name aloud. "Who was the other victim?"

"*Alleged* victim," Edwards finally felt compelled to interject. "I should probably mention Mr. Kincaid is presumed innocent."

Judge Carpenter sighed but managed not to roll his eyes. "Of course, counsel. Alleged victim. And who was the other alleged victim?" he asked Brunelle.

"Her name was, uh," he needed a moment, "Ashleigh Engel."

"Ah," Carpenter responded. The names didn't mean anything to anyone, of course. It was just important that they were different. "Well, then, let's proceed. Ms. Edwards, have you received the charging documents? Do you waive a formal reading?"

"Yes, Your Honor," Edwards answered. "We have received copies of the charging documents, waive a formal reading, and ask the court to enter a plea of not guilty to the charge."

"A plea of not guilty will be entered," Carpenter confirmed. "Conditions of release, Mr. Brunelle? I assume this is more of a formality, since the defendant hasn't managed to post bail on his other case yet."

Brunelle could feel Edwards getting angrier. "I don't know about that, Your Honor. I would just ask the Court to set bail in the same amount as the previous case: one million dollars. And all the same conditions as well, to include no contact with any surviving family of the alleged victim, uh," he glanced at the charging documents, "Stephanie Pang."

Judge Carpenter nodded, but at least pretended to consider any argument from the defense. "Ms. Edwards?"

"The Court is correct that Mr. Kincaid has been unable to post the one million dollar bail set on his other case," Edwards said. "That being the case, we would ask the Court not to set bail on this case. He's obviously not going anywhere. Doubling his bail would serve no legitimate purpose."

"It would keep him from killing anyone," Carpenter suggested, not very neutrally.

"First of all, Your Honor," Edwards snapped at the

judge, "this new charge predates the other charge, so that comment isn't even factually appropriate. More importantly, it's legally inappropriate. Mr. Kincaid is presumed innocent and he's entitled to every benefit of that presumption, including a judge who actually believes he might be innocent."

Carpenter looked suitably chastened. "I apologize, Ms. Edwards. That comment was less than judicial. What I meant to say is that the Court has considered the allegations, your client's criminal history, and all other relevant factors; the Court believes that your client is a risk to reoffend and poses a danger to the safety of the community; and therefore bail is set at one million dollars. Is that better, Ms. Edwards?"

Edwards sneered. "Thank you, Your Honor," she managed to say through gritted teeth.

"Anything else," Judge Carpenter asked, "before we move on to the next case?"

Brunelle looked to Carlisle who responded with a thoughtful shake of her head. Then he looked at Edwards, to see if the defense had anything.

"That depends," Edwards responded. "Is Your Honor also hearing criminal motions, or just doing arraignments?"

Carpenter hesitated, trying to glean the meaning behind the question. "Just arraignments. Motions are assigned out to one of the other judges. Frankly, Ms. Edwards, I would have expected you to know that."

"Just confirming, Your Honor," Edwards replied as she pulled a pleading out of her file and handed copies to the bailiff and Brunelle "I would hate for someone as obviously impartial as Your Honor to be troubled with the defendant's motion to sever Mr. Kincaid's cases for separate trials. I'm glad to know it will be heard by a different judge."

Carpenter didn't smile. He also didn't take the paper offered to him by his bailiff. He simply said, "Very good," then called out, "Next case!"

Brunelle stepped back from the bar to review Edwards's pleading with Carlisle as Edwards herself stepped back to confer briefly with her client before he was taken away by the guards so the next defendant could be brought in.

"Not surprising," Carlisle said as she pulled the document from Brunelle's grasp. "She said she was going to do this."

"Right," Brunelle agreed. "I think she was going to try to spring it on us and try to get a ruling at arraignment. But Carpenter wasn't going to be the best judge for her."

Carlisle handed the pleading back to Brunelle and raised her gaze as Edwards approached them.

"That went well," Carlisle teased. "For us, I mean."

"For me too," Edwards replied. "At least I don't have to worry about 'Presumed Guilty' Carpenter deciding my motion to sever."

"I don't want to be *that* prosecutor," Brunelle said, "but your guy is actually guilty. He said so himself. In fact, he's way more guilty than just the two murders we can prove."

"You think you can prove," Edwards returned. "If I win, you'll have two separate razor-thin cases. Odds are good he walks out of King County Jail when this all ends, no matter how much bail you put on him now. Why don't you just let him plead guilty and we can all be done with the case?"

"Cases," Carlisle corrected.

"See?" Edwards grinned and pointed at Carlisle. "Even Gwen thinks I'm going to win the severance motion."

"I think you're going to lose the cases," Carlisle said. "It doesn't matter how many trials we have to do."

"But that's just it," Edwards said. "It does. This is all such a colossal waste of time. You caught him. He'll pled guilty. Why are we even doing this?"

"Because he killed two women, Jess," Brunelle answered. "More than two. A lot more, according to him. It wouldn't do them justice if he got out of prison after only fifteen years."

"Oh, don't pretend like you care about those women," Edwards scolded. "You couldn't even remember their names without looking at your paperwork."

"I care," Brunelle insisted. "It's my job to care."

"If it's your job," Edwards laughed, "then you don't really care. You didn't know them. You never met them. You have no idea what kind of people they were."

"It doesn't matter what kind of people they were," Brunelle responded. "They didn't deserve to be murdered."

"No argument there," Edwards said. "And I've offered you a way to hold my guy responsible without getting all holy crusade on me. If you don't want to take it, fine. But don't pretend like you care. You don't. Not really. No one does."

Edwards stormed away before Brunelle could think of any further comebacks.

"I mean, she's not wrong," Carlisle offered. "It's just not relevant. These were women with no friends and no family and that's why Kincaid targeted them. It doesn't matter if no one cares. We still have a job to do."

Brunelle frowned as he listened. "But I do care," he insisted.

Carlisle nodded and put a hand on Brunelle's shoulder. "No, you don't, Dave. Not really," she echoed Edwards. "No one does."

Carlisle turned toward the exit as well and Brunelle followed, distracted, as he considered whether he really cared. He thought he did. But maybe Edwards and Carlisle were right. Maybe he only cared because he was paid to care. In which case he didn't really care. And if he didn't care, then they were right— no one did.

"Excuse me." An Asian man a little older than Brunelle approached them as they stepped into the hallway. He was holding the hand of an Asian woman about his same age. Both were dressed up and both looked very sad. "We just saw you in court. You are the prosecutors on the Stephanie Pang case, correct?"

Carlisle nodded but let Brunelle answer.

"Yes, that's right," he confirmed. "Who are you?"

"I'm Arnold and this is Eleanor," the man answered. "We're Stephanie's parents."

CHAPTER 25

A pair of stunned looks and one short elevator ride later, Brunelle and Carlisle found themselves sitting down in Brunelle's office with the parents of murder victim Stephanie Pang.

"Thank you for taking the time to meet with us," Arnold Pang started.

Brunelle was only too happy to meet with a victim's family. He just didn't understand why he didn't know about them before. Usually part of any case was outreach to the family. Maybe they just assumed no one cared. And now he had to pretend like he wasn't surprised by their sudden appearance at the arraignment.

"Of course, of course," Brunelle answered. "An important part of any case is meeting with the family. Thank you for coming to court today."

He was hoping that might spark exactly how they knew about court, but neither Arnold nor Eleanor addressed that unspoken question.

"Of course we came to court," Eleanor said. "Stephanie

was our daughter, no matter what she ended up doing with her life."

And that was enough of an opening for Carlisle to pounce. Or start to ask questions. That's how lawyers pounce.

"Tell us a little more about that," Carlisle said. "How much did you know about Stephanie's lifestyle? How long had that been going on?"

Eleanor looked at her husband, who returned a pained look and squeezed her hand.

"We don't really like to talk about that," Arnold said. "It went on for too long. That's enough."

Brunelle wasn't that sure it was enough, but he was hardly going to press the point on their first meeting.

"We did everything we could to help her," Eleanor insisted. "But the drugs, they were too powerful. It was just so dangerous. And so shameful."

"We didn't let her stay with us when she was on the drugs," Arnold explained. "We had to have rules. We couldn't have that going on in the house, you know?"

"Of course, of course," Brunelle agreed.

"She would stop by sometimes," Eleanor went on, "when she needed money for drugs. Then she would just disappear. We hadn't seen her for a very long time, and we were starting to worry."

"Then we saw in the papers," Arnold picked up, "that someone had been arrested for murder. The article didn't print her name, but they gave a description and we knew it was her. We just knew. So, we came to court today to see for sure."

Eleanor took a tissue out of her purse and dabbed her eyes. "We didn't want it to be her. But we knew it was."

"When you said her name out loud in court," Arnold

said, "we knew for sure. Stephanie Pang."

"Our Stephanie," Eleanor sobbed into her tissue.

It was awkward. Awkward because there was nothing Brunelle or Carlisle could do to bring the Pangs' daughter back. And awkward because it was confirmation that Brunelle didn't really care after all. Not like these people. He understood what Edwards was trying to say. But she wasn't completely right. He might not be able to feel the depth of loss and despair Stephanie Pang's parents were feeling right then, but he wasn't indifferent to it either. He had chosen his career for a reason. He did care, at least generally. Arnold and Eleanor Pang could care specifically.

"We're very sorry for your loss," Brunelle offered. "And I can promise you that we're going to do everything we can to hold Stephanie's killer responsible."

Carlisle nodded along to both sentiments.

"Oh, please, yes," Eleanor reached out and grabbed Carlisle's hand. "Please do that. I know our Stephanie wasn't perfect. She made some bad decisions. She did some bad things. But she was sick. And she was trying. She didn't deserve to be murdered like that."

"No one does," Carlisle agreed. "We'll make sure the man who did this pays for it."

Brunelle was a little uncomfortable with that promise. Especially with the evidentiary problems of their cases. No one could ever really promise anything in a criminal case—except to try their best. So that's what he did.

"We'll do our absolute best," Brunelle hedged. "Stephanie deserves that much."

"Thank you," Eleanor said with another dab at her eyes.

"Yes, thank you," Arnold echoed. He stood up and extended his hand. "That's all we can ask for."

As Brunelle stood up to shake Arnold's hand, he felt compelled to be honest with the poor couple. "I do have to tell you," he said. "This isn't the strongest case I've ever had. We know it was him, but we don't have any witnesses, and we don't have a confession. It's circumstantial, based on forensic evidence and the opinions of experts. We can't promise we'll win."

Arnold frowned and looked at his wife, who returned his expression. Then he nodded and turned back to Brunelle and Carlisle. "We understand. Just promise us you'll try. You'll do your best. You won't cut him any deals or let him out early. Try your best to hold him responsible for killing our Stephanie. That's all we ask." ·

That was a lot to ask, actually. But Brunelle knew he spoke for Carlisle when he answered. "We will. I promise."

It was a solemn moment, between grieving parents and those who would seek to allay that grief. But it was interrupted by joyful squeals and angry shouts. A young girl, not more than six, ran into Brunelle's office, followed quickly by an elderly Asian woman, who was followed less quickly by Brunelle's legal assistant, Nicole.

"Papi! Gram-gram!" the little girl shouted, and she ran over to hug the Pangs, an arm around one leg each.

"Oh, I am so sorry," said the woman chasing after the girl. "She just wouldn't stop asking to see you, and they said we could come back, but then she ran ahead. I'm so sorry."

Brunelle waved off the apology. "No worries. We were finished anyway."

Arnold turned the little girl around to face Brunelle and Carlisle. "This is Emily. Stephanie's daughter."

Eleanor smoothed Emily's hair and smiled. "This is why

we care so much," she said. "We need her to know that's there's good in the world. We need her to know that there's justice in the world, even for the lowest among us."

Brunelle smiled back and nodded. "That's a pretty good reason to care," he said. "And I promise, we'll do everything we can."

Brunelle might not have been able to care deeply about the death of someone he'd never met, but that didn't mean he didn't care about anything.

He cared about justice.

CHAPTER 26

"So, you didn't promise them anything?" Emory asked that night after Brunelle had gotten home and they'd opted for a night in of takeout and Netflix. She was sitting on the couch, he was laying down with his head on her lap, and the TV was showing whatever the latest recommended series was. Something set in outer space, but where most of the astronauts went around in sports bras and underwear. "Not even to make them feel better?"

"Their daughter's dead," Brunelle responded. "Nothing I say is going to make them feel better."

"I don't know, man." Emory shook her head. "Something like, 'We'll make the bastard pay' might have made them feel pretty good."

"Maybe," Brunelle answered, "right up until the jury says 'not guilty' and those two words hurt even more because that stupid prosecutor promised them a guilty verdict he doesn't actually have any control over."

"You have some control over it," Emory argued. "You put on a good case; you give a great closing argument; you look all reliable and official in that suit of yours. That gives you some control over it."

"That gives me influence over it," Brunelle corrected. "Not control. Big difference."

Emory snorted. "You lawyers and your word games. You know what I mean."

"And I know not to promise something I only have influence over," Brunelle said. "Under-promise and over-deliver, remember?"

"I don't know," Emory said. "That's a lawyer thing. Cops, we want to over-promise and over-deliver. We want to catch the bad guys and put them away where they can't hurt anyone anymore."

"I want that too," Brunelle agreed. "I guess I just got blindsided. I wasn't ready to meet the family. Oh my God, that little girl?"

"You like kids?" Emory asked.

"I don't hate them."

"I don't want kids," Emory said quickly.

"Yeah, me either," Brunelle agreed. "But the point is, I didn't think there was any family—not any that cared anyway."

"It's good that someone cares," Emory said.

"I care too," Brunelle insisted. "Really."

"I know," Emory answered, running her fingers over his head. "But Edwards is right, too. You don't care like that. And it's okay. You shouldn't."

"I shouldn't?"

"No," Emory said. "That would be weird."

Brunelle laughed. "Wow. Thanks."

"Care enough to do your job well," Emory went on, "but it begins and ends there. Have you ever gone to a funeral for one of your victims?"

Brunelle thought for a moment. "No."

"Have you ever been invited to any type of memorial service for one of them?"

"No," Brunelle admitted. "I got a thank you card once. No, twice. And like a button thing with the victim's name on it."

"After the case was over?"

"Yeah, afterward," Brunelle agreed.

"See, you're the bad penny," Emory explained. "No one wants you around. You're the reminder of the bad thing, the missing thing, the life cut short by murder. I mean, we're all going to die—"

"Why does everyone keep saying that?" Brunelle interrupted.

"It's true," Emory answered.

"Sure, but I don't want to keep thinking about it," Brunelle complained. "And I definitely don't want to keep talking about it."

"The homicide prosecutor doesn't want to talk about how everybody dies eventually?" Emory laughed.

"Not everybody dies by homicide," Brunelle pointed out. "I'm just dealing with one small subgroup of death. I don't need to think about the other groups."

"Maybe it would make you a better prosecutor?" Emory suggested.

"Nope," Brunelle answered.

"A better person?"

"Nope again." He took her hand from where she was stroking his hair and held it against his chest. "I'm already perfect."

"You're okay," Emory allowed.

"Just okay?" Brunelle asked.

"Very okay," Emory said.

"That doesn't really improve it," Brunelle said. "It just kind of deepens the mediocrity of it."

"I know."

"You know?" Brunelle asked.

"I know," Emory squeezed his hand against his heart. "And that's why I like you."

Brunelle froze for a moment. They hadn't used the L-word yet. He figured it would happen in the throes of passion, or whatever, when either or both of them could later disavow it. Not laying on the couch, sober, watching some terrible sci-fi series. That made it real. Irrevocable.

"Just like?"

"Very like," Emory teased.

Brunelle squeezed her hand back and reached his other up to touch her cheek. "I very like you, too."

CHAPTER 27

They could have drawn a better judge for the hearing on the motion to sever/join the cases for trial. In fact, Brunelle thought as they made their way to Judge Findlay's courtroom, they probably couldn't have drawn worse.

Judge Marcus Findlay had been a public defender for thirty years before running for and being elected to the Superior Court. He was suspicious of cops and even more suspicious of prosecutors. Thirty years of practice was long enough to see at least one cop lie and deal with at least one prosecutor who played dirty. In Brunelle's mind, those were one-offs, the exceptions that proved the rule. For Marcus Findlay, those were just the ones who were stupid enough to get caught.

Still, he was no friend to murderers either. Not anymore anyway. But then, who was? Edwards, Brunelle supposed. And Saxby. Neither of whom were in the courtroom when Brunelle and Carlisle entered at exactly 8:59.

"That's weird," Brunelle commented. "Jessica is usually early. She's annoying like that."

"She's annoying in more ways than that," Carlisle

responded. She nodded toward the defense table. "Kincaid isn't here either. Maybe we have the wrong day."

Kincaid wasn't there because the corrections officers were keeping him nearby in a secure holding cell until the bailiff called for him, and the bailiff wasn't going to call for him until Edwards arrived.

"Are we in the right courtroom?" Brunelle joked as he and Carlisle made their way down to the prosecution table.

"Maybe we got a different judge," Carlisle whispered hopefully.

Brunelle kept his smile as he whispered back, "Don't complain about the refs. Just play the game to win."

"Really?" Carlisle rolled her eyes. "A sportsball metaphor? Don't be such a dude all the time."

Brunelle thought for a moment. "I'm not sure how to be anything else."

Carlisle finally smiled and slapped him on the back as they reached their counsel table. "Maybe that's your problem."

Brunelle wasn't sure what point Carlisle was trying to make, except that it didn't seem to have anything to do with whether Kincaid's two murder cases should be tried together or separately. So, he addressed his next comment to the bailiff, who had ignored his earlier quip about being in the right courtroom.

"We are in the right place, right? Judge Findlay. Nine a.m. Motion to join trials."

The bailiff looked up from her computer screen, then at the clock, then finally at Brunelle. "Yes, you're in the right courtroom. Where is defense counsel?"

"Am I my opponent's keeper?" Brunelle joked.

The bailiff's expression became even more stone-faced, if

that were possible. "You don't know either, then?"

"Um, no," Brunelle coughed. "We don't know either."

"Well, this is annoying," Carlisle huffed as they spread their materials out on the prosecution table. "I don't want to get cold before my argument."

"Yeah, about that," Brunelle raised a thoughtful finger. "I was thinking maybe I would do the oral argument after all."

Carlisle raised an eyebrow. "I wrote the brief," she pointed out.

One of the perks of being the senior attorney was making the junior attorney write the briefs. That was especially good when the junior attorney generally wrote better briefs than the senior attorney. She also argued motions really well. But ultimately, it was the senior attorney's case.

"The thing is," Brunelle began, rubbing the back of his neck, "this is a really important motion, maybe the biggest one we'll face on these cases. I don't want Findlay to think we don't understand how important it is. I'm afraid he'll think we don't really care if I'm not the one arguing it."

"Because you're a man?" Carlisle challenged. "A straight white man, with flecks of gray and a red power tie, just dripping in cis het male privilege?"

"I didn't even understand that last bit you said," Brunelle looked down at his attire. "I'm not sure what my tie has to do with it."

"You're really just proving my point," Carlisle grumbled. "You do realize at least that much, don't you?"

Brunelle dodged the question. "Look, I'm lead counsel. Everything we do sends out a subtle signal. Judges know that junior attorneys argue the motions that don't matter as much, to get experience. And they know that the senior attorneys argue the biggest motions, the ones that really need to be won. We've already got two strikes against us with how thin these cases are and drawing Findlay to hear the motion. We need to scrape up any advantage we can."

"And you think having you argue the brief I wrote," Carlisle asked, "is an advantage?"

"I think the lead attorney standing up to argue tells the judge that we think this is serious," Brunelle answered. "And yes, that's an advantage."

Carlisle crossed her arms and stared at Brunelle, her mouth twisted into a knot and her foot tapping audibly on the floor. After several taps, she uncrossed her arms and threw them up in the air. "Fine. You're lead counsel. You just said so. So, it's your decision. Good luck. Hit a touchdown, or whatever. I'll sit here and cheer you on. I should have brought my pom-poms."

"You have pom-poms?" Brunelle tried to diffuse the tension with another joke.

But Carlisle wasn't having it. She just pointed at him and said, "Don't."

Brunelle followed her advice. He looked at the clock on the wall. 9:10. He turned to the bailiff again. "When do we strike the hearing?"

"Or better yet," Carlisle chipped in, "call out the judge and let us argue our side. If Edwards isn't here by the time we're done, we win. That's better than just striking it, because she can't raise it again if we get a ruling on the merits."

"Not sure it's on the merits if the other side doesn't argue," Brunelle pointed out.

"Fine, then on our merits," Carlisle said. "Or rather, my merits, since I wrote the brief."

"We won't be striking the hearing, or proceeding without Ms. Edwards," the bailiff said. "At least not until Judge Findlay determines how to proceed. He will take the bench at nine-fifteen if Ms. Edwards still isn't here, and we can address the matter on the record."

Brunelle frowned and turned away. "That's a lot less fun," he muttered to Carlisle.

"So is sitting by while someone else argues your motion," she responded.

Brunelle was about to repeat his arguments in support of him arguing the motion when Edwards burst through the courtroom door, her coat over one arm, her other arm pulling a rolling briefcase behind her. And behind that briefcase came Saxby.

"Sorry I'm late!" Edwards called out, as she rushed toward the front of the courtroom. "Go ahead and call for Mr. Kincaid. We're ready!"

"Nice of you to show up," Brunelle remarked as Edwards dropped her coat on her chair and yanked her briefcase onto the table, its rolling handle still extended.

Edwards grinned at him. "Oh, you know how it is, Dave. There are always so many angles to play and just not enough time to play them all."

Brunelle wasn't at all sure how it was. *What angles?* he wondered. But before he could say anything, Judge Findlay took the bench.

"All rise!" bellowed the bailiff. "The King County Superior Court is now in session, The Honorable Marcus Findlay presiding!"

Edwards tugged at her suit coat even as Judge Findlay ascended to his seat above them. Brunelle took a moment, then straightened his own tie, and waited for the judge to address them.

Findlay was older than he looked; he had to be with that much experience. He still had a full head of thick hair, although it was completely white, and his eyes were bright and sharp, with no glasses blocking them from view. He had a neatly trimmed white beard that stopped at a thin neck which suggested a trim figure beneath the amorphous black robe.

"Ah, I see everyone is here now," Judge Findlay remarked first. Obviously, the bailiff had kept him informed of the morning's events. "Call for the defendant."

Brunelle and the rest of the lawyers remained standing as the bailiff picked up the phone, whispered into it, and a few moments later a secure side door to the courtroom opened with a clank. One corrections officer entered, followed by Kincaid in jail garb and handcuffs, followed by a second corrections officer. They marched him to his spot at the defense table between Edwards and Saxby. Edwards whispered something to the nearest corrections officer, who nodded in return, then unlocked Kincaid's handcuffs. Kincaid rubbed his wrists as he looked around the courtroom. He finished his scan at Brunelle, his lips peeling back into a broad and cold grin.

"Are the parties ready to proceed?" Judge Findlay asked once Kincaid was settled in with his attorneys.

"The State is ready," Brunelle answered.

"The defense is ready as well, Your Honor," Edwards responded.

Brunelle cursed himself for forgetting the 'Your Honor.' *Everything we do sends out a subtle signal.* He hoped Findlay hadn't noticed. He knew that he had.

"Before we get started," Findlay said, "I want to advise

the parties that I am fully prepared for this hearing. I have read the charging documents for both cases and the factual summaries provided by the State to support those charges. I have read both sides' briefs. I have read every case cited in those briefs, and every other case that cites to those cases. Unlike some other judges, I do not need you to educate me on the law. I need you to persuade me as to my ruling."

Brunelle was glad to hear that. There were definitely judges on the bench who either didn't know the law, or worse, didn't understand it. A lawyer could spend valuable time and energy just trying to educate a judge as to what the law was before even being able to explain how it applied in the particular case before them. But a judge who knew the law and read the briefs? That was a relief. Doubly so when Brunelle would be arguing off of someone else's brief. Findlay had basically just invited him to go off script and sell him the State's position, rather than simply recite the arguments in the brief. Which was good, since he hadn't written the brief. He was ready for that. But he didn't get to go first.

"This has been filed as a defense motion to sever cases for trial," Judge Findlay continued, "although I didn't see anything in the record to indicate they had ever actually been joined for trial."

"Defense counsel filed her motion at arraignment, Your Honor," Brunelle offered by way of explanation. "So we never got to the issue of joinder."

Findlay nodded for several seconds at Brunelle, then turned to Edwards. "Ms. Edwards, why don't I let you explain why you filed a motion to sever before the cases were actually joined, if I'm reading the docket correctly."

"You are, Your Honor," Edwards confirmed. "And Mr.

Brunelle is right, in part. We did file the motion to sever at the arraignment, but we did so after the State advised us, off the record, of their intent to join the cases for trial."

"Is that true?" Findlay asked Brunelle. Both he and Edwards were still standing; everyone else had sat down.

"Yes, Your Honor," Brunelle answered. "We are not contesting that it was our intent to join the cases for trial. We would like to get a ruling on the merits, so we are not making a procedural argument that Ms. Edwards's motion to sever is premature because they haven't been formally joined yet."

Findlay frowned at that. He reached over and picked up a document to his right. "'State's Response to Defendant's Motion to Sever'," he read aloud. "'Section One: The defendant's motion is premature because the cases have not yet been formally joined for trial'." He looked up at Brunelle. "Are we all here for the same case? Is there another Michael James Kincaid accused of murdering two different people on different dates and at different locations? Am I in the wrong courtroom, Mr. Brunelle?"

Brunelle took a moment before responding. First, so he didn't say anything out of embarrassment or anger. Second, to make absolutely sure he should say what he was about to say. "My apologies, Your Honor. Ms. Carlisle wrote the brief, and I'll be deferring to her for the oral argument from here on out."

With that, he gestured for her to stand and quickly sat himself down.

Carlisle hesitated, but only in order to process what Brunelle had just said for a moment. After that moment, she was on her feet. "That is correct, Your Honor. Trials cannot be severed until they are actually joined. The Court should first join the cases for trial, and only then consider the defendant's motion to sever. The State believes when the Court does this, the Court will see that a joint trial promotes not only judicial economy but a full and fair determination of the matters at issue."

"You mean," Findlay simplified it, "whether Mr. Kincaid is guilty of these two murders, correct? Those are the only questions that would be put to a jury, if I understand how trials work."

"Correct, Your Honor," Carlisle responded. She was smart enough not to keep talking. Findlay clearly liked talking, and if there was one thing a person who liked talking didn't like, it was other people also talking.

The judge looked to the defense table. "What say you, Ms. Edwards? Is your motion premature?"

Edwards shrugged. "I don't know, Your Honor. Maybe," she conceded. "But we're short on time, and I think it's a mistake to get hung up on procedure. The issue before the Court is whether these two separate murder charges should be joined for trial and decided by the same jury. I don't think they should. Whether I argue against a motion to join or argue in favor of a motion to sever is really just semantics. The issue is what's fair to Mr. Kincaid, and that is never premature."

Judge Findlay stared at Edwards for several seconds. Then he put his hands together in front of his mouth and nodded. "I can't argue with that, Ms. Edwards. I can't argue with that." He clapped those hands together. "All right then. I will hear first from Ms. Edwards. You were the one who noted this motion and your brief was filed first, so it makes sense to let you lead. The floor is yours, counselor."

"Thank you, Your Honor," Edwards responded, taking a moment to center herself as Carlisle sat down to wait her turn.

"This," Edwards gestured vaguely toward the prosecutors, "is nothing more than a naked attempt at bootstrapping, in the desperate hope of stealing a conviction where none should lay."

Brunelle raised an eyebrow at the formalistic turn of phrase. But he admired Edwards's passion. It was easier to do that knowing he wasn't the one who would have to stand up and match that passion when she'd finished.

"The State has filed two extremely weak cases against Mr. Kincaid," Edwards continued. "I would call them paper thin, but that would be an insult to paper. They are tissue thin. Membrane thin. Alone, each case would fail. Together, they should still fail, because the evidence will be just as weak, but what jury would be strong enough to acquit a defendant of two murders? That's the real reason the State wants to join these cases for trial, and that's the strongest reason to sever them. To join them would be to tempt the jurors to violate their oath to hold the State to its burden. It's hard enough for a jury to acquit someone once the State has filed charges and put all of its reputation and prestige behind the mere fact of charging the crime in the first place. Add to that the State's allegation that the person has done it before, and no jury could withstand that pressure."

Brunelle wasn't sure *no* jury could withstand that pressure, but he could hardly deny that he wanted that extra pressure on them.

"Imagine instead," Edwards continued, "that these cases were to be tried sequentially, one right after another. Imagine the first jury heard all of the evidence on the first case—what little evidence there is. And imagine they followed their oath, and held the State to its burden, and came out of their deliberations ready to deliver a verdict of 'Not Guilty'. Now imagine, before we let them announce their verdict, we tell them, 'Wait. Before you tell us how you voted, we wanted to tell you one more thing. He's also accused of this other murder. Does that change your verdict?' And we all know it would. We all know that, at a minimum, they would pull that verdict form back and want to know more about this second murder. Even though they had made their decision properly based on the evidence and the law, they might change their verdict based on just the allegation of a second crime. Now, imagine they got all the evidence of the second case—just as weak, but still there— and it's not hard to imagine them crossing out that 'Not' on the first verdict form, even though the State's evidence was the same as to that crime when they were ready to acquit."

All very hypothetical, Brunelle thought. Not inaccurate, but still, very hypothetical.

"We exclude evidence of other crimes all the time, Your Honor," Edwards continued. "Evidence Rule 609 excludes almost all prior convictions, unless the defendant testifies as the conviction is for a crime of dishonesty, like false reporting or perjury. Evidence Rule 404(b) excludes all prior bad acts, with very limited exceptions to prove things like motive or identity. Indeed, the Evidence Rules are based on the understanding and acknowledgement that jurors are only human, and humans have biases and prejudices that have no place in a court of law. In the particular arena of criminal law, the biggest prejudice we encounter is the belief that someone is more likely to have committed the crime in question if they committed similar crimes in the past. That may be a useful supposition in everyday life, but in here, in the courtroom, that belief would relieve the State of their burden to prove each and every element of the instant crime beyond a reasonable doubt. And so those prior crimes are and rightly should be inadmissible."

Edwards paused for a moment to take a drink from her water bottle. Brunelle took the opportunity to glance at Carlisle to appraise her apparent readiness to respond to Edwards. She was staring straight ahead, hands folded, capped pen nowhere near the notepad she could have been using to note Edwards's more salient points. Yep, she was ready.

"There is no good reason not to have two trials, Your Honor," Edwards continued. "The government has the resources. We have the judges and the courtrooms. We have the prosecutors and the jurors. We have myself and Mr. Saxby. We're not going anywhere, and we're more than prepared to defend Mr. Kincaid against these charges, time and again if need be, but in a setting that is fair and doesn't relieve the State of its burden.

"We can and should conduct a separate trial for each of these charges," she continued. "And when we do, we can ensure that justice is done for each case, individually, whatever that outcome may ultimately be. But if these cases are joined for trial, there can be no justice. No jury would acquit Mr. Kincaid no matter how thin the State's evidence is. And it is thin, Your Honor. Membrane thin.

"Let each case stand or fall on its own merits," Edwards implored." We're not afraid of that. The State shouldn't be either. But they are, and that tells you everything you need to know. Safeguard justice, Your Honor. Sever these cases. Thank you."

"Should I applaud?" Brunelle whispered to Carlisle as Edwards sat down.

"Hush," Carlisle snapped back in her own whisper. "It was a good argument. If you can't admit that, you can't beat it."

"Thank you, Ms. Edwards," Judge Findlay said. "Excellent advocacy." He turned to the opposing counsel table. "Ms. Carlisle, your response?"

"Thank you, Your Honor," Carlisle said as she stood to address the judge. "And I agree. That was excellent advocacy by Ms. Edwards. And it underlines how important a decision this is for the parties in this case. I know Your Honor takes that responsibility seriously, and so I will endeavor to address Ms. Edwards's concerns and further, to explain the affirmative reasons why a joint trial of these allegations is not only the practical decision, but the one that actually optimizes the quest for justice."

Nice intro. Brunelle frowned approvingly.

"I regret to say that I do disagree with Ms. Edwards regarding procedure," Carlisle continued. "I believe it is important that the Court first consider whether to join the cases for trial, and only then consider whether they should be severed. The criteria for joinder are slightly different from those for severance, and a careful consideration of the relevant factors at the appropriate times in the inquiry will show why these cases should be joined for trial."

Brunelle fought the urge to reach for the court rule handbook. It had been a while since he'd actually looked at the exact language of the rules governing joinder/severance. That was one of the dangers of becoming experienced—you started to think you knew everything and stopped looking things up.

"Joinder of charges is governed by Criminal Rule 4.3," Carlisle said. "That rule states that offenses may be joined for trial when they are of the same or similar character, even if not part of a single scheme or plan, or are based on the same conduct or on a series of acts connected together or constituting parts of a single scheme or plan. Here, the crimes are clearly of the same or similar character. Both cases involve an allegation that the defendant selected a random victim, working as a prostitute, murdered her, then disposed of the body in an out of the way location. Indeed, the bodies were found not a quarter of a mile apart. Those similarities alone are sufficient to join the cases for trial.

"But those similarities are more than just similarities. Rather, they are evidence that the crimes, the murders, were based on a series of acts connected together, constituting a single scheme or plan. What was that single scheme or plan, Your Honor may ask? Why, to murder as many women as possible. And that plan required above all else that he not be caught before he could kill again. Here, we have dump sites in very close proximity and DNA from one victim found in the vehicle observed driving away from the disposal of the second victim. So, looking to the text of the rule, joinder is proper, and the Court should join the cases for trial."

Carlisle took a moment to catch her breath, and to let her arguments sink in a bit with Judge Findlay. Brunelle was prepared to give her a 'You're doing great' but Carlisle didn't look down at him before starting up again.

"Now, once the cases are joined for trial, and only then, the Court can consider severance. Severance is governed by Criminal Rule 4.4. That rule offers little guidance, however, stating only that the Court shall grant severance if the Court determines that severance will promote a fair determination of the defendant's guilt or innocence as to each offense. This is essentially Ms. Edwards's argument, but she does little more than assert that no jury could ever be trusted with the knowledge that the defendant may have committed more than one murder. She argues that any such jury would violate their oaths and ignore the Court's instruction to decide each case separately. Indeed, there is a standard criminal jury instruction that will tell them to consider each count separately and that their decision on one count cannot influence their decision on any other count. The fact that this standard instruction exists is important for two reasons. First, it shows that joint trials are common enough to need a standardized instruction, and second, we believe jurors can actually follow this instruction and follow the law and their oaths. I believe that as well."

Another pause, another breath, another opportunity to look at Brunelle to see how he thought she was doing, another instance where she did no such thing.

"What Ms. Edwards fails to mention is that the danger she seeks to avoid is, in fact, unavoidable. The jury will hear about both murders even in separate trials, and the relevant case law makes clear that joint trials are favored where the evidence in one case would be cross-admissible in the other case. That is, if we were going to have to put on most of the case surrounding the discovery of Ashleigh Engel's body in order to prove the case regarding Stephanie Pang anyway, then there is no prejudice to having the jury decide both cases. And that is exactly what will happen here. We can't explain to the jury how we discovered Stephanie Pang's DNA in the defendant's vehicle without putting on evidence that links him to Ashleigh Engel's murder as well. Two trials would be duplicative and therefore a waste of resources. And the jury that will decide whether the defendant is guilty of the murder of Stephanie Pang will also know that he is accused of the murder of Ashleigh Engel."

Brunelle could tell Carlisle was about to wrap up, and he was genuinely interested in how she was going to push her argument over the goal line.

"In fact, Your Honor," she jutted a finger into the air, "the real danger for Mr. Kincaid comes from having separate trials. If he has a joint trial, then the jury that decides his fate will be told, and repeatedly told, that he is presumed innocent of both charges against him and that the State has the burden of proving each and every element of each and every offense beyond a reasonable doubt. However, if the Court severs the cases and separate trials are held, imagine the situation if he is convicted in the first trial. Then, when we present our case to the second jury, they will hear not only that he was accused of another murder, they will hear that he was convicted of it. If Ms. Edwards is truly worried what a jury will do if given the knowledge there is more than one crime, I can think of no greater prejudice than the jury knowing the defendant is already guilty of one of them."

Brunelle looked over at Edwards. She seemed genuinely irritated by that argument. Brunelle thought it was pretty good too.

"So, Your Honor, in conclusion," Carlisle summed up, "I urge the Court to address the concerns of both parties, remember that a joint jury will be told the defendant is presumed innocent of both charges, and do the one thing that will, in fact, promote a fair and just determination of the defendant's guilt as to each separate case. Deny the motion for severance and set these cases for a joint trial. Thank you."

Carlisle sat down again, and Brunelle finally had a chance to whisper, "Great job!"

Carlisle nodded in acknowledgement, but she kept her eyes trained on Judge Findlay.

The judge was shifting his weight, clearly

uncomfortable. "Yes, well," he began, "this is a very important decision, as Ms. Carlisle stated at the outset of her argument. As I said when I took the bench, I have read all of the materials associated with this case, including but not limited to the briefs filed by both sets of attorneys. While I appreciate Ms. Carlisle's precision in wanting the Court to first decide on joinder, then on severance, I think we can all agree the decision comes down to, as Criminal Rule 4.4 states, what will promote a fair determination of guilt or innocence of the defendant as to each offense. The easy answer would seem to be severance. Separate trials would eliminate most of the concerns we might have about a jury being overwhelmed by the gravity of there being two alleged murders instead of just one. On the other hand, the evidence in these two cases is undeniably intertwined, and I do find it hard to imagine trying either case without at least some mention of the other."

He paused and tapped his index fingers against his lips. "And I think that ultimately, that is what controls my decision. That, and a point brought up by Ms. Carlisle which I have to admit I had not considered before. If I order separate trials, and if the defendant is convicted at the first trial, then the fact of that conviction would almost certainly make its way to the jury in the second trial. If Ms. Edwards is concerned, and rightly so, that a jury would be swayed by a mere accusation of murder, then I can see no way they would not be swayed by a conviction for murder, especially for a murder whose evidence is enmeshed with the murder charge they are trying to decide."

The former public defender turned judge gave a heavy sigh. "Therefore, I am going to grant the State's motion to join these two cases for trial, and I am going to deny the defendant's motion to sever."

Carlisle finally looked at Brunelle. "And that is why you let me argue the motion," she said.

"But there is one more thing," Judge Findlay announced. "The rule on severance contemplates that the defense will renew its motion for severance at the close of the State's case-in-chief. In fact, as we all know, if the motion to sever isn't renewed, the issue is waived on appeal. That means I fully expect Ms. Edwards to raise this issue again at the appropriate time."

Uh-oh. Brunelle was afraid he knew where Findlay was going with all that.

"I'm not sure the trial judge could rule fairly on that motion," Findlay continued, "without having heard the original arguments for and against severance put forward today."

Yup. Brunelle was right. *Crap.*

"Therefore," Findlay concluded, "rather than return this case to criminal presiding for assignment for trial, I am going to preassign the case to myself. I will be the trial judge so I can rule on the severance motion when it is raised again mid-trial."

"Shit," Carlisle hissed.

"Agreed," Brunelle whispered back.

"I will see everyone again in four weeks," Judge Findlay announced, "Court is adjourned."

Findlay stood up and retreated to his chambers. Brunelle and Carlisle stood up as well and started gathering their things. Drawing Findlay for the trial notwithstanding, the ruling on severance was a huge victory, but they would have to wait until they were up in his office before they could celebrate. Professionals don't rub it in their opponents' faces.

But they do extend a handshake and a 'good job' to opposing counsel, once their client can't see them being nice to each other. So, once Edwards was done with her immediate post-ruling debrief with Kincaid, and the corrections officers had re-handcuffed him and led him out of the courtroom, Brunelle crossed over to the defense table, extended his hand, and said it. "Good job, Jess."

Edwards took his hand and shook it. She was a professional too. "I'm really sorry, Dave," she said.

"It's okay, Jess." Brunelle responded. "We can handle Findlay for the trial. After all, he ruled in our favor on the motion."

"Oh, I'm not sorry about any of that," Edwards explained. "I'm sorry about why I was late."

Brunelle didn't like the sound of that. A quick glance at Carlisle's expression confirmed she didn't like the sound of it either.

"Why were you late?" Brunelle asked.

"I went over your head, Dave," Edwards answered. "I had to. While you were down here getting ready for the hearing, I was upstairs talking to your boss. I asked Matt Duncan directly to accept our plea offer."

CHAPTER 28

Brunelle stormed off the elevator and headed straight for Duncan's office. Carlisle shared the elevator ride but didn't seem to be trying to keep up with him. That was just as well. He didn't really want her to be a part of the confrontation that was about to happen, but he didn't tell her to wait outside either. She wasn't really one to be told what to do. Then again, neither was Duncan, but there they were.

"Is he in there?" Brunelle asked Duncan's personal assistant, even as he strode past her desk without breaking stride.

"He's on the phone," she responded. "You can't go in there."

"It's okay." Brunelle grabbed ahold of the door handle. "I'm pretty sure he's expecting me."

Brunelle pushed open the door and marched inside.

Duncan was at his desk, leaning back in his chair, phone to his ear. When he saw Brunelle, he sat up again. "I'm going to need to call you back," he said into the receiver, then hung it up.

"Dave, how nice of you to barge in announced."

"It's my case, Matt," Brunelle fairly barked. "You gave me thirty days to pin another murder on Kincaid, and I did it. You can't accept their offer."

Duncan nodded slowly. "First of all, I absolutely can accept their offer. I'm the Elected Prosecutor and your boss. Second, why didn't you tell me there was a new offer on the table?"

"Because I already rejected it," Brunelle answered. "There was no need to get you involved."

"I beg to differ," Duncan responded. He stood up and walked around to lean on the front of his desk. Brunelle was still standing by the door, back straight and fists clenched. "I said you could reject his first offer if you found a second murder. I didn't say anything about subsequent offers. You should have come to me."

"What did you tell her?" Brunelle demanded.

"Who? Edwards?" Duncan clarified.

"Yes. What did you tell her? Gwen and I just won the motion to join the cases for trial. Don't tell me that was all for nothing."

"I told her I'd think about it," Duncan answered. "And congratulations on winning the motion."

"I don't want your congratulations, Matt," Brunelle said. "I want you to back me up. I want you to tell Edwards no."

"I'm not sure no is the right answer, Dave," Duncan replied. "Even if you did win your motion to join. There are a lot of factors to consider."

"And none of them compare to putting a serial killer away for the rest of his life," Brunelle shot back. "That's the only thing that matters, Matt."

Duncan frowned slightly and pointed at Brunelle. "Yes, but are you sure you can do that?"

"I'm sure I'll do everything I can," Brunelle offered. "And so will Gwen."

"I know that already, Dave," Duncan responded. "Hell, I'd be disappointed with anything less. But it may not be enough."

"Don't take the offer, Matt," Brunelle pleaded. "Just don't."

"Or else what?" Duncan challenged his subordinate.

Brunelle thought for a moment before going ahead and saying it. "Or else I'll quit. I won't amend the charges down. I won't. I'll quit first."

Duncan tipped his head slightly and crossed his arms. "Be careful, Dave. I know you care about this case, but you're talking about throwing away your entire career. You've worked too hard to get where you are to throw it all away over one case."

"Two cases," Brunelle corrected. "And really it's probably more like twenty. I can win this trial, Matt, and I'll be damned if you're going to take it away from me."

Duncan's patient expression finally melted away. "Are you sure about this, Dave?"

Brunelle wasn't sure he was really sure, but he said it anyway. "Yes, I'm sure."

Duncan nodded for several seconds, then uncrossed his arms and pointed at Brunelle again. "Okay, Dave, I'll tell you what. I won't accept their offer. I'll let you try the case. But if you lose…"

"Yes?"

"If you lose," Duncan finished, "I will accept your

resignation."

Brunelle felt his heart drop into his stomach.

"Do we understand each other?" Duncan asked firmly.

Brunelle nodded, his jaw clenched, his gut on fire. "Yes, sir."

* * *

When Brunelle emerged from Duncan's office, he found Carlisle there, standing outside Duncan's door. She fell into step with him as he stomped past.

"What did Duncan say? Did he accept Kincaid's offer?"

"I convinced him to say no," Brunelle answered.

"What did it take to do that?"

Brunelle stopped walking and looked down. "Maybe everything."

"What does that mean?" Carlisle asked as she came around to stand in front of him.

Brunelle took a beat, then looked up at his partner. "It means we have a lot of work to do. We have to win this trial."

CHAPTER 29

Brunelle had a routine he followed the night before trial. Traditionally, it involved being alone and calming his mind over a single glass of 10-year-old Kentucky bourbon. More recently, that traditional glass of bourbon had turned into two glasses shared with Casey Emory. But traditions were made to be broken, and the day of the night before trial made Brunelle want to share that glass of bourbon, not with a new love, but with an old friend. Someone he could truly tell anything.

"Larry!" Brunelle called out as Chen entered the bar around the corner from Brunelle's condo. He waved the detective over to the table he had snagged in the back corner.

Chen made his way through the bar and took the high stool opposite Brunelle at the small table with its one candleholder and two drink menus. "Hey, Dave. Thanks for inviting me. I can't stay long, though. Evie doesn't like it when I'm late for dinner. Shouldn't you be home soon too? Trial starts tomorrow."

"I know, I know." Brunelle raised his hand to get the attention of a server. "One round. I just needed to talk with someone before the trial starts."

The server came over and took their drink orders. Brunelle had that bourbon, but Chen ordered a Dr. Pepper. He couldn't just walk around the corner to his place.

"Why not Casey?" Chen asked. "You haven't screwed that up already, have you?"

Brunelle frowned at Chen. "No. What do you mean 'already'? You know what, never mind. No, this." He pulled a letter from his coat pocket. "I got this at the office today. There's no return address, but we both know who it's from."

Chen took the envelope and pulled out the single sheet of paper inside. As he unfolded it, Brunelle could see the page in his mind, the only thing on it a simple four-line poem, the words written in dull pencil because inmates weren't allowed access to ballpoint pens:

> *When the verdicts are read,*
> *"Not Guilty" times two,*
> *I'll do it again,*
> *And it's all thanks to you.*

"Wow," Chen said after reading it aloud. "He's taunting you."

"Yeah," Brunelle said. "Just makes me all the more determined to put him away for good."

"Can you link it to him?' Chen asked. "It's sort of a confession."

Brunelle shook his head. "I doubt it. He didn't sign it, and there's no return address. I can prove it came from the jail, but I've got a few defendants sitting in the jail right now."

"We could run it for prints," Chen suggested.

"He's not that stupid," Brunelle said what Chen was already thinking too. "It's easy to avoid leaving fingerprints, especially when someone else will get theirs all over it before they realize not to."

Chen nodded. "Still, it seems a little cocky to me. You may find a chance to shove it back in his face."

"And down his throat," Brunelle added. "I hope."

"Is this what you wanted to talk about?" Chen asked. "I mean, I don't mind a drink with an old friend, but this seems like it could have been an email. Or a phone call, anyway."

"No, there's more," Brunelle admitted. The server arrived then with their drinks. Brunelle took a sip from his, then said, "I kind of told Duncan I'd quit if I didn't win the trial."

Chen nearly spat out his mouthful of Dr. Pepper. "What? Why the hell would you do that?"

"Well, actually I threatened to quit if he accepted Kincaid's updated offer," Brunelle explained. "He agreed not to accept the offer, but told me I'd better win the trial, or he'd accept my resignation."

"You threatened him like that?" Chen asked. "You know he's your boss, right? And this is just one case? You can't throw away your entire career over one case."

Brunelle frowned. "That's what Duncan said. I may have already done it, though. I probably should have told him about the updated offer."

Chen's eyebrows raised. "You didn't tell him?"

"No. I mean, why should I? I already rejected it."

"Did you tell him that?"

"Yeah." Brunelle nodded.

"That's why he said he'd accept your resignation," Chen

said. "You can't just disregard him like that."

"He would have taken the offer, Larry," Brunelle said.

"Probably," Chen agreed. "Maybe. Who knows? But you need to let him make that call."

"Isn't that what *I'm* paid to do?" Brunelle asked. "We don't run all our cases past him. There's too many for that."

"Yeah, but he was already involved," Chen pointed out. "I don't know, man. That sounds like you lost your head a little bit. What did Gwen say when you told her?"

"Uh, well, I didn't actually tell her." Brunelle shrugged. "I just told her we needed to win the case."

Chen frowned at Brunelle. "What about Casey? Did you tell her?"

Brunelle shook his head. "No. She doesn't need to know that kind of stuff."

"Okay, see, that's what I was talking about when I asked you if you'd screwed up your relationship with her yet," Chen chided. "You can't keep that stuff from your girlfriend, Dave. You think losing your job won't impact your relationship? Wait until she finds out you didn't tell her in advance. You have to tell her, man."

Brunelle nodded at his friend's advice, but didn't agree to follow it. Instead, he asked, "How do you do it, Larry? How do you work case after case and not get burned out? You even got shot and came back for more. How do you care enough to do the job right, but not too much to screw it up?"

Chen thought for a moment. "Well, I guess that's the job, right? That's what I signed up for when I decided to be a cop. Just like you did when you decided to be a prosecutor. It's who I am."

Brunelle nodded. "It's who I am, too."

"Well, then," Chen looked him in the eye. "You'd better win this case. Because if you lose, you don't get to be that person anymore."

CHAPTER 30

There was a routine for the first day of trial too. Mostly it just involved reporting to the right courtroom and hoping you'd done enough to be ready for what was to come.

When Brunelle had been a baby prosecutor, his cases were shoplifting, driving under the influence, and low level assaults. Important, but, if he was honest, not that important. Certainly not important to anyone except the officers and victims directly involved in the particular incident. But as he gained experience and worked his way up the crime ladder, his cases became more serious, the stakes higher for those involved, and the drama of it all more interesting to those not involved. Once he reached the top rung, murder, he could expect the courtroom to be filled with at least the victim's family members, maybe the defendant's family members, and definitely junior attorneys who wanted to learn a thing or two from the older generation. Or at least wanted to see them slug it out.

So, when Brunelle and Carlisle walked into Judge Findlay's courtroom that morning, they encountered several members of the local criminal bar, about half of whom were rooting for them. They also saw Arnold and Eleanor Pang. But no one was there for Ashleigh Engel. Or Michael James Kincaid.

Brunelle and Carlisle greeted the Pangs on their way to begin setting up their things on the prosecution table. Nothing complicated. Definitely no promises. Just "Hello" and "Thank you for coming" and "Let us know if you have any questions".

Edwards was already there, along with Saxby and Kincaid. Kincaid was dressed for court in a dark suit and red tie. Jurors weren't allowed to know a defendant was being held in custody pending the outcome of the trial. It might impinge on the presumption of innocence. The three corrections officers guarding every exit might have given it away, but otherwise Kincaid just looked like a fifth lawyer in the room.

Brunelle wondered what that said about lawyers.

There were preliminary matters to attend to before the trial could actually start. Mostly clarifying what evidence would or would not be admissible at trial. Nothing too contentious. Complicated motions to suppress evidence were supposed to be handled prior to trial, kind of like the motion to sever trials.

The other big task was selecting the jury. That would take the better part of a day, maybe two, depending on the panel of prospective jurors. As it was, the prospective jurors weren't all that interesting. Mostly teachers and engineers— people whose employers paid them even while they were on jury duty. No one else could afford to take off the weeks needed to sit on a murder jury. Everyone agreed to follow the law. No one knew Kincaid or any of the attorneys. A few of them didn't like cops or The System, and Brunelle struck them. A few didn't like criminals and believed in Law and Order; Edwards struck them. When they were done, the jury box held twelve bland citizens without strong enough opinions to be too offensive to either side. And once they were selected, sworn in, and ready to go, Judge Findlay said to them, "Ladies and gentlemen, please give your attention to Ms. Carlisle, who will deliver the opening statement on behalf of the State of Washington."

CHAPTER 31

Carlisle stood up and stepped out from behind the prosecution table. A large part of their trial preparation had been selecting who would do what. Mostly, who would examine which witnesses, but also who would give opening statement and who would give closing argument. It was important each of them did one of those, not have Brunelle do both. It was his case, technically, but they were partners, and they wanted the jury to know it. Brunelle wanted to do closing, so that meant Carlisle got to do opening. Which was fine by her. It meant she got to talk first.

Normally, a lawyer will stand somewhere generally directly in front of the jury box to deliver opening statement. Or at least to begin it, although one might move around a bit after starting. But Carlisle turned her back on the jurors and walked over to stand in front of the defense table. She turned around to face the jurors again, then pointed directly at the suited Michael James Kincaid.

"He doesn't look like a serial killer, does he?"

That's what they called 'a hook.'

Edwards called it an objection. She slammed to her feet. "Objection, Your Honor!"

Which was probably the exact reaction Carlisle was hoping for. She sauntered away from the defense table to that more traditional spot in front of the jury box as Edwards made her argument. Or tried to.

"Counsel is appealing to the emotions of the jury," she tried. That was sort of a basis for an objection. Lawyers weren't supposed to do that. But it was a murder trial. A double murder trial. It was going to be emotional. The best lawyers were the ones who weaved their emotional appeals invisibly into their legal advocacy. Although, Brunelle had to admit, that gambit wasn't particularly invisible.

Findlay wasn't impressed by either Carlisle's theatrics or Edwards's objection. He declined to rule on the objection, and instead just told Carlisle to "Move on, counselor."

Carlisle was happy to oblige.

"Serial killer," she repeated the phrase. "How many murders do you have to commit before you're a serial killer? Three? Ten?" She paused, as if considering her own question. "What about only two murders? What if you get caught after the second one, and the investigation uncovers the first one?"

Carlisle walked over to the defense table again and looked directly at Kincaid. "Yeah, that makes you a serial killer," she said. "And Michael James Kincaid is a serial killer."

Edwards resisted the urge to object again, although Brunelle could see she wanted to. Still, it might make the jury think she was worried about what Carlisle was doing. So, instead, she tried to look nonchalant as the prosecutor hovered over her table accusing her client of being the worst humanity had to offer.

"But let's not talk about him just yet," Carlisle said as she stepped back toward the jury box. "I want to tell you about someone else. Two someone elses, in fact. Let me start by telling you about Ashleigh Engel."

Carlisle nodded at Brunelle, who stood up and walked over to the document projector sitting on a stand between the two counsel tables. Another part of trial prep had been working out the choreography of the opening statement Carlisle was going to give. He took a photograph off the counter in front of the bailiff where all the exhibits were laid out and placed it on the projector. A moment later an enlargement of Ashleigh Engel's driver's license photo was displayed on the white wall opposite the jury box. There was no family to give them a more candid in-life photograph.

"This is Ashleigh Engel before she met the defendant," Carlisle said. "She was twenty-eight, born and raised right here in Western Washington. She was also a drug addict and paid for her habit through acts of prostitution."

Sad, but true, Brunelle thought. *And relevant.*

Carlisle nodded at him again, and he switched out the driver's license photo for another photograph, one far less appealing than even a DMV photo. A moment later the white wall opposite the jury was filled with a close-up of the mound of maggots that covered Ashleigh Engel's face upon the discovery of her body.

"And this is Ashleigh Engel," Carlisle said over the gasps and retches of the jury, "after she met the defendant."

Hearing the stifled sobs of Eleanor Pang behind him, Brunelle was suddenly grateful that there was no one there for Ashleigh. That kind of advocacy might have been a bit too much, even for the righteous purpose intended.

It was a risky way to give an opening. The photo was gross. It was upsetting. The risk was that the jurors, or some of them anyway, would be upset at Carlisle for forcing them to see it. But the odds were, as mad as they might be with her, they would, and should, be even more angry at Kincaid.

"This is what she looked like when she was discovered by the police," Carlisle continued, then corrected herself. "Actually, she wasn't discovered by the police. She was discovered by a literal junkyard dog. A dog that dug under the fence and came back with a human bone in his mouth. Ashley Engel's arm bone."

Several of the jurors cringed at that. *Good*, thought Brunelle.

"The night watchman saw what the dog had dragged home and called the police," Carlisle continued. "The cops responded and after a brief search, they located her body. She had been outside for a while and decomposition was advanced." She glanced one more time at the photo still on the wall. "That's why there were so many maggots."

She nodded a third time to Brunelle, who removed the photo and turned off the projector light, then returned to his seat.

"But the thing about those maggots," Carlisle explained, "is that they aren't just stomach turning. They're useful. Believe it or not, they can be used to calculate with a high degree of certainty exactly when a body has been dumped and exposed to the elements. And that's what was done in this case. You're going to hear testimony from a forensic entomologist who will explain that using information like the type of fly species native to the area and the daily temperatures for the relevant time period, he was able to determine almost the exact time the defendant dumped Ashleigh Engel's body behind the abandoned pet food warehouse next to the junkyard.

"Then you'll hear from Seattle Police Detective Larry Chen," Carlisle continued. "He was the lead detective on this case, and using the information from the forensic entomologist, he pulled the security video from the junkyard. The cameras caught the defendant driving behind the warehouse, then speeding away a few minutes later. And the video captured his license plate number as he sped past the front of the junkyard."

Carlisle paused at that moment to catch her breath and let her words sink in with the jury. She also took a moment to look back at Kincaid, which had the desired effect of pulling the eyes of more than a few jurors to the defendant. Edwards was still looking forcibly nonchalant. Kincaid, though, was staring a hole through Carlisle.

"Detective Chen used that vehicle information and located both the defendant and his vehicle," Carlisle went on. "The police executed a search warrant, looking for any evidence related to the murder of Ashleigh Engel. The search didn't turn up anything definitive regarding Ashleigh, but they did find some blood drops in his trunk. The DNA was examined. It wasn't Ashleigh's, but it was female. And so the search was on for a possible second victim."

Brunelle was feeling good about their decision to have Carlisle do the opening statement. She was an engaging speaker, and she was unfurling the story in a way that seemed to be keeping the jurors interested. It probably didn't hurt that it was the first time they were learning what the case was really about. Still, she was doing a great job papering over the fact that they didn't actually have very much evidence against Kincaid.

"Police focused on recent unsolved murders and missing

person cases," Carlisle explained, "especially those with victims similar to Ashleigh Engel. They were looking for cases that were close in details. They didn't necessarily expect to find a case close in distance too. But not more than a few hundred yards south of where Ashleigh Engel's body was recovered, investigators found a second set of human remains."

Brunelle didn't need the nod from Carlisle to know to stand up again and grab the photographs of Stephanie Pang from the exhibit counter.

"This was Stephanie Pang before she met the defendant," Carlisle said as Brunelle put up a photo Stephanie's parents had provided of Stephanie smiling outside near some flowering trees. Then Brunelle swapped out that idyllic scene for a cold shot of a skull in the mud. "And this is Stephanie Pang after she met the defendant."

Carlisle paused again to let the jurors compose themselves. In some ways, the image was less troubling than the pile of maggots they had seen before, but there was something visceral about seeing a skull. It was an absolutely unmistakable symbol of death.

"Not only was her body dumped in the same vicinity as Ashleigh Engel's," Carlisle said, "but the way she was murdered was identical. You're going to hear from the medical examiner who conducted the autopsies, and she's going to tell you that Ashleigh and Stephanie both died from a single gunshot wound to the left side of their heads."

She took a beat, then summarized it again for any of the jurors who might not have gotten it the first time around. "Same occupation. Same location. Same manner of death. Same killer." She pointed again at Kincaid. "Same serial killer. The defendant, Michael James Kincaid."

Carlisle took a deep breath, then clasped her hands in front of her as she took a half step toward the jurors. "I'd like to take a moment to speak about these women's occupations. Sex workers. Prostitutes. Hookers. Whores. I wouldn't just like to speak about it. I need to. It's important you understand two things.

"First, their occupations don't matter. Those women didn't deserve to be murdered, and I find it a little bit enraging that I even have to say that out loud. If any of you have any doubt about that, leave right now. Raise your hand and tell the judge you have no business sitting on this jury. Then get out of that jury box because you don't deserve the honor of sitting there."

Aggressive, Brunelle had to admit, but there was no doubt how she felt.

"Second, their occupations matter a great deal. These women were targeted because of what they did to stay alive. I'm not saying the defendant was on some sort of psychotic crusade to murder sinners and wrongdoers. No, I'm saying the defendant needed someone he could overpower. Someone who would get into a car with a stranger and go to a remote location to commit a crime. They just didn't know the crime would be their own murder."

Carlisle gave Brunelle one last nod, and he returned two photos to the projector, one of each victim, both while they were still alive.

"Ashleigh Engel and Stephanie Pang," Carlisle said. "You're going to hear us say their names a lot in this trial. They aren't just faceless victims. They were real people. Real, living, breathing human beings. Until they met the defendant.

"They deserve to have their names said aloud.

"They deserve to have a voice.

"And at the end of this trial, we are going to stand up again and ask you to give them that voice. We are going to ask you to return verdicts of guilty to two counts of murder in the first degree. Thank you."

Carlisle lowered her head for a moment, then walked briskly back to her seat next to Brunelle.

"Excellent," he whispered to her out of the corner of his mouth.

"I know," she whispered back. "Now shut up."

Her eyes were fixed on Edwards, who was standing up even as Judge Findlay told the jurors, "Now, ladies and gentlemen, please give your attention to Ms. Edwards, who will deliver the opening statement on behalf of the defense."

CHAPTER 32

Edwards offered a brief "Thank you" to the judge as she walked up to the jury box. Her posture was noticeably relaxed, almost slouched. Brunelle thought she seemed almost... bored? Definitely not formal. But he knew it was intentional. Everything is intentional when you're in front of the jury.

"Wow," she started, with a wave toward the prosecution table. "That was terrible. Am I right? Those two poor dead women?"

The jurors seemed a bit taken aback as well, although they only had Carlisle's hard-nosed style to compare her against.

"Oh, don't worry," Edwards assured the jurors. "I'm not going to show you those photos again. Those were horrible. Oh, and unnecessary. We're not contesting those women were murdered. We're just saying the State won't be able to prove Mr. Kincaid did it. In fact," she threw an almost pitiful glance at Brunelle and Carlisle, "they can't prove anyone did it."

She turned back to the jurors and utilized the same sincere clasped hands gesture they teach in trial advocacy classes. "You see, they don't have any evidence. That's why they put those photographs up there. They want you to see and remember those pictures. They want you to get angry. Then they want you to be angry at whoever they put in that defendant's chair over there. They don't care that there's no evidence. Or rather, they do care, and that's why they don't want to talk about it."

It actually was objectionable to question the motives of opposing counsel, but Brunelle wasn't about to look that thin-skinned. He kept pretending to take notes. Carlisle continued to stare at Edwards, as if studying her every word and move—which Brunelle knew was exactly what she was doing.

"Look," Edwards said collegially, "here's what really happened. They found a body. They guessed at the time it might have been left there, using crazy fake bug science. Once they guessed a date, they pulled nearby surveillance video and saw a car drive by. They grabbed a still and zoomed in to get a grainy, low resolution license plate number they think belongs to Mr. Kincaid. They seize his car and search it. And you know what they find? Nothing. Nada. Zero. Not one darn thing related in any way to the body they found."

She shook her head and looked disapprovingly at the prosecutors, before turning back to her real audience. "Now, you may be thinking, 'What about that other case? The prosecutor said there was DNA in his car from that one.' And that's true; Ms. Carlisle did say that. But just because a lawyer says something, that doesn't mean it's true. Just the opposite, right?" she joked, a bit awkwardly given the situation. "But seriously, the judge is going to tell you, what the lawyers say is not evidence, and you are absolutely required to disregard any remark, statement, or argument by an attorney that is not supported by the evidence. So, just keep an open mind."

She took a moment and nodded, mostly to herself.

"Keep an open mind," she repeated. "Wait and see what the evidence actually shows. Wait and see what they can actually prove. And when the evidence is all in and they haven't proved anything after all, the only possible verdict will be not guilty, times two."

Brunelle's head shot up even as Edwards thanked the jurors and turned back to the defense table.

'Not guilty times two'

She knew about the poem. She fucking knew. But Brunelle didn't have time to do anything about it.

"The State may call its first witness," Judge Findlay instructed.

CHAPTER 33

Putting on a trial was essentially just telling a story. But in the worst possible way. Multiple storytellers, each with only part of the story, having to answer specific questions instead of being allowed to just tell what they know, and constantly being interrupted by someone who doesn't want the story to be told. Oh, and the listeners didn't even want to hear the story; they were threatened with jail if they didn't show up.

But still, a story. And given that the listeners weren't there by choice, it was a good idea to make it as easy as possible for them. The easiest way to tell a story was chronologically. Something so mundane might not win any literary awards, but the only award Brunelle cared about was a one-word verdict at the end of the trial. One word, times two.

The truly first witnesses to the story were unavailable. Ashley Engel and Stephanie Pang were dead, and they weren't allowed to call Kincaid as a witness. That left Jared Unger, the night watchman at Nextdoor Junkyard, Inc., guarder of junk, feeder of Dobermans, retriever of tibias, caller of 9-1-1.

Unger wasn't a complete stranger to the criminal justice system, although it might have been his first stint as a witness rather than a defendant. He had more than a few misdemeanor convictions, mostly criminal traffic and a disorderly conduct. The kinds of things you might expect from somebody who couldn't find a better job than night shift security guard at a junkyard. But he cleaned up pretty well and looked downright respectable in a white dress shirt and khakis as he entered the courtroom and made his way to the front to be sworn in by the judge.

Once he'd sworn to tell the truth, the whole truth, and nothing but the truth, Unger sat down on the witness stand and waited for Brunelle to ask him the first question. He was a little on the heavy side, with short black hair, and beads of sweat betraying an otherwise calm appearance.

"Could you please state your full name for the record?" Brunelle started with the usual first question as he stepped out from behind the prosecution table.

"Jared Jason Unger," he answered, a touch of nerves in his voice.

"How are you employed, sir?" The usual follow-up question to the usual first question.

"Um, I'm a loss prevention officer at the Dollar Shack," Unger answered, almost apologetically.

Brunelle was a bit surprised by the answer, as was the jury, he imagined. But it wasn't his first rodeo, or trial. "Is that a relatively new job?"

"Yes, sir," Unger confirmed.

"Did you previously work at a different business?" Brunelle suggested. "Perhaps on West Marginal Way in the southern part of Seattle?"

Brunelle wasn't allowed to feed the actual answer to Unger—that would be leading the witness—but he could do everything short of that.

"Yes," Unger seemed relieved to say. "I was a security guard at the Delaney and Sons' Salvage Yard in White Center."

Okay, back on track, Brunelle let out a small sigh of relief. No one likes a story that takes forever to get to the good stuff. The jurors didn't care about Unger's resume; they wanted to hear about the bone.

"Okay, great," Brunelle acknowledged the preferred response. "So, what shift did you work there?"

Unger shifted in his seat. He seemed eager to tell his part of the story, but Brunelle wasn't making it easy. Another problem with the storytelling procedure: the person in charge of presenting the story wasn't allowed to ask questions that included any part of the story. "Um, I worked a lot of different shifts. But, I mean, I worked the graveyard shift too, if that's what you're asking."

That was definitely what Brunelle was asking, even if he wasn't allowed to ask it specifically.

"It is, thank you," Brunelle affirmed. "And did something unusual happen one night when you were working the graveyard shift? Something that led to you calling the police?"

"Um, yeah," Unger laughed slightly, mostly out of nervousness, but a bit out of the absurdity of it. "One of our dogs found a human bone."

Another problem with the storytelling model could occur when the designated storyteller, the witness, wasn't very good at it. When he didn't take the time to build up the story, but instead just blurted out the ending. So, Brunelle pressed rewind.

"Let's back up a little," Brunelle signaled to Unger, and the jury. "Could you tell us a bit about where Delaney and Sons' Salvage Yard is located, and what other businesses or buildings are nearby?"

"Right." Unger nodded. He started trying to use his hands to explain. "Okay, see, Delaney's is right here. Then, to the left—well, left if you're looking at the street, but right if you're looking at the building. I think that's south. North? No, south, I'm pretty sure."

Brunelle gestured toward the large pad of paper on the easel behind the witness stand. "Perhaps you could draw us a map?"

Unger exhaled audibly. "Yeah, that would be a lot better. Thanks."

He stood up and walked to the easel, picking up the black marker resting on the front edge of it. It took him a few minutes to draw everything he thought might be relevant. He was a bit of an artist even, and finished with a cartoon dog holding a cartoon bone in its mouth.

Brunelle took the time to casually appraise the jury. They seemed engaged, although he would hope so on only the first witness. Still, Unger was affable and likeable enough, good traits for a first witness. It set the tone and hopefully made the jury more likely to trust the prosecution, more likely to believe the story.

"Okay," Unger announced that he'd finished his drawing. "So, this is Delaney's, this is West Marginal Way, this is the river out back—I think it's the Duwamish River maybe? Anyway, there's a river behind the fenced-in lot out back."

"Okay," Brunelle echoed. He pointed to the map from

his spot in front of the witness stand. "And those other squares, are those other businesses?"

"Um, kinda," Unger answered. "They're other buildings, but I don't think they're businesses anymore. Everything is pretty much shut down and abandoned down there. That was part of why I found a new job. It was depressing. Well, that and the whole thing with the dog finding a human arm bone."

"Yes, let's go ahead and talk about that a little more." Brunelle took the opportunity to move the story along. "Please retake your seat on the witness stand, and then tell the jury how that unfolded. Did you know the dog had gotten out, or did he just show up with the bone in his mouth?"

Unger returned the marker to its tray and sat down again in the witness chair. "Well, I didn't notice she was missing," he started to tell Brunelle.

But Brunelle pointed to the jury. "Tell them," he instructed. This was the interesting part of the testimony. Brunelle wanted Unger to be looking at the audience as he delivered it.

"Oh, okay." Unger hesitated, then turned to face the jurors. "So, I didn't notice she was missing or anything. I mean, they stay out in the yard in case someone tries to climb the fence or something, and I stay inside watching the security cameras. I do a walkaround of the yard every hour or so and when I went to do my one a.m. walkaround, I saw Ginger—that's the dog's name—I saw Ginger just sort of laying in the corner, facing away, and making like a weird noise. I thought maybe she was sick, because usually they come right up to me. Honestly, I didn't really like that part of the job. They're really big dogs, but they're super well trained, so I guess I was always safe. But still, Dobermans. Anyway, JoJo—the other dog—she came right up to me like usual, but Ginger didn't, so I went over to see what was up."

"And what was up?" Brunelle encouraged.

"An arm bone," Unger answered Brunelle, then remembered to look at the jury. "An arm bone," he repeated to them. "With like some of those little carpal tunnel hand bones still stuck to it, and I think a finger still attached. It was pretty gnarly, actually. I felt like I was gonna puke."

"Did you take the bone away from the dog?" Brunelle asked.

"Did I take a bone away from a Doberman chewing on it?" Unger raised his eyebrows at Brunelle, then turned again to the jurors. "Uh, no. No, I did not try to take a bone away from a Doberman."

A few of the jurors chuckled. That confirmed they liked him. Mission Accomplished. Brunelle just needed to wrap it up and sit down.

"What did you do instead?"

"I went back inside and called nine-one-one," Unger answered.

"Did you ever leave the business and try to see where Ginger got the bone from?" Brunelle asked.

"No, sir." Unger was looking at Brunelle again when he answered, but that was fine. The important part was over. "I did look around the yard later and saw where she dug under the fence in the back. I'm thinking she could smell the body and kinda went crazy to get to it."

Gross, Brunelle thought, *but probably correct.*

"What happened when the police arrived?" Brunelle pressed toward the finish line.

"I told them what I found," Unger said. "Or what Ginger

found, I guess. They called animal control who showed up and helped them get the bone away from Ginger, or what was left of it anyway."

"Did just one police officer show up?" Brunelle knew the answer but needed Unger to tell the jury.

"Oh, no," he said. "It was a whole team. Like a squad, or whatever. Cop cars everywhere, lights flashing, the whole bit. And they were there for a long time too. They were still there when I finished my shift at six a.m."

"Did you ever go over and look at the body?" Brunelle asked.

"No, sir," Unger answered. "Not interested. It was gross enough what I did see. I didn't need to see more."

"So, after telling the cops what you, or what Ginger found," Brunelle wrapped up, "did you do or observe anything else related to the investigation?"

"No, sir," Unger answered definitively. He could tell that was the last question, and he was obviously glad for it.

"Thank you, Mr. Unger," Brunelle said. Then to Judge Findlay, "No further questions, Your Honor."

Brunelle returned to his seat next to Carlisle. Edwards stood up and approached the witness stand, even as Judge Findlay asked her, "Any cross-examination?"

"Yes, Your Honor," she answered. "Briefly."

She squared up in front of Unger. "I just have a couple of questions, Mr. Unger. They may seem silly, but don't worry, I'm not trying to trick you."

Unger's eyebrows knitted together a bit. "Uh, okay…"

"You don't know when the person whose arm bone you saw actually died, right?" Edwards asked.

Unger thought for a moment. "Uh, right."

"You never saw that person at or near Delaney and Sons, correct?"

"Correct," Unger agreed a bit more readily. "I mean, not that I know of."

"And you never saw whoever it was who put the body there, correct?" Edwards continued.

"Right," Unger agreed.

"In fact, to be absolutely clear," Edwards said, "you have no idea who the dead person was, when she died, who put her body near your former place of employment, or when they did that, correct?"

"Correct."

"You just saw a dog chewing on an arm bone and called the cops, right?" Edwards summarized.

"Right." Unger nodded.

"And so you never saw my client," Edwards pointed at Kincaid, "at or near Delaney and Sons at any time that might be relevant to this case, correct?"

Unger thought for a moment. "Uh, no. I've never seen your client before at all."

Edwards smiled and nodded. "Thank you, Mr. Unger. No further questions, Your Honor."

Findlay looked down at Brunelle. "Any redirect examination, counsel?"

Edwards hadn't done any damage. Everything Unger said was true. He was the spark that started the investigation, but he couldn't speak to how Kincaid was identified. There was nothing to rehabilitate and asking questions just to get the last word would make it look like Edwards had hurt his case somehow. Brunelle stood up. "No, Your Honor. Thank you."

Findlay turned to Unger. "Thank you, sir. You are

excused." Then the judge looked to Brunelle again. "The State may call its next witness."

"Thank you, Your Honor," Brunelle answered. "The State calls Detective Larry Chen of the Seattle Police Department."

CHAPTER 34

Chen was Brunelle's witness too. Generally, Brunelle and Carlisle were going to try to trade off witnesses, so the jury got to see both of them. That's why Brunelle did the first witness after Carlisle's opening. But Brunelle was at the crime scene with Chen, so he'd know if something was missing in Chen's descriptions. Plus, Brunelle and Chen were friends; they had a good energy between them. It was important for the jury to see that. Anything to make Brunelle more likeable.

Chen entered the courtroom and walked purposefully to be sworn in. He was wearing a brown blazer and dark pants, with his badge clipped to his belt. His expression was somewhere between professional and disinterested. Jared Unger was new at being a witness, but Larry Chen was an old hand. It wasn't boring, but it wasn't exciting either. Just another part of the job.

In a few moments, he was sworn in and seated on the witness stand, ready for Brunelle's first question.

"Larry Chen," he answered that same usual first question, followed by the answer to that same usual second question, "I'm a detective with the Seattle Police Department."

"How long have you been a detective?" Brunelle asked.

"Over twenty years now," Chen turned to tell the jurors directly. Like all professional witnesses, he'd been trained to give his answers directly to the jury. "A long time."

The jurors liked that. Chen was down to earth, real. And he was really the narrator of the story. Brunelle was the MC, the guy who welcomed you, thanked you for coming, reminded you to turn off your phones, and urged you to tip your waitresses. But it was Chen who was going to tell the jury the lion's share of the story. So, it was important the jurors liked him, found him credible, believed his story. Down to earth and real was perfect for that.

"What unit are you assigned to?"

"I've been a detective in the homicide unit for seven years," Chen answered. "Prior to that, I was assigned to the major crimes unit."

Brunelle nodded and stole a quick glance to check the jury. They all seemed engaged. Good. Time to get back to the story.

"Were you involved," he asked, "in the recovery of a homicide victim in the area of Delaney and Sons' Salvage Yard on West Marginal Way in Seattle's White Center neighborhood?"

"I was," Chen confirmed.

"How did you come to be involved in that?"

Chen turned again to the jury. "Dispatch received a call, a report of human remains. Apparently, a guard dog at the salvage yard brought back a bone from the victim, so the night watchman called nine-one-one. Patrol responded first, but whenever there's a possible homicide, one of us detectives gets called too. It was my night to be on call, so I got the call."

"So, you went out to the scene?" Brunelle followed up.

"Yes." Chen nodded.

"Had the rest of the body been located when you arrived?"

"No, not quite," Chen answered. "But the patrol officers were already canvassing the area. I started talking to the security guard, a man named Unger, but within a few minutes, I got word that the patrol guys had found her."

"What did you do?"

"I broke off the conversation with Unger and went directly to the body," Chen explained.

Brunelle nodded. "Could you please describe the area where the body was located?"

"Sure," Chen agreed. He turned to the jurors again. "The body was located behind the abandoned pet food warehouse next to Delany and Sons, in a narrow wooded strip between the gravel parking lots and the Duwamish Waterway."

"And what was the condition of the body?"

Chen frowned. "Um, I would say it was in an advanced state of decay. I estimate it had been outside at least two weeks, maybe three."

"Objection!" Edwards stood up and reminded everyone she was there. "This witness doesn't have the expertise to estimate time of death. He's not a pathologist."

Brunelle was fine with that objection. It set up the next witness perfectly, the actual expert on time of death.

"I'll concede the objection," Brunelle offered, which meant Findlay didn't have to rule on it and Edwards could sit down again. "Detective Chen," he said, "don't estimate the exact time of death, but can you say, based on your own experience as a homicide detective, that the body had been outside for more than just a few hours?"

"Yes," Chen answered. "I can definitely say that."

"Why?"

"The maggots," Chen told the jurors.

Brunelle took a moment and retrieved the photograph from Carlisle's opening statement. Edwards had made it seem like they were trying to shock a conviction out of the jurors. And there was some truth to that. But he wasn't going to back down in the face of her accusation. He wasn't going to let her make him change his game plan. Well, that wasn't entirely true—he was already contemplating a shift in witness order. But he was definitely going to show them that picture of the maggots.

Once it was up on the wall again for all to see, Brunelle turned back to Chen. "Why did the maggots matter?"

"That's a lot of maggots," Chen observed. "That doesn't happen in just a few hours. Not even a few days. That told me the body had been out for a while. And that was important."

"Why was that important?"

"Because I needed to find out who put the body there," Chen explained. "I needed witnesses. But I needed to know when it happened in order to know who might be a witness."

"Were you able to determine, that night, exactly when the body had been dumped?" Brunelle asked.

"That night?" Chen clarified. "No."

"Were you able to determine it later?"

"Not personally," Chen answered, "but we retained an expert to determine it."

"And what did the expert determine?"

Edwards was on her feet again. "Objection. Calls for hearsay."

Brunelle knew she was right. Normally one witness can't testify to what another witness said or concluded. But there were exceptions. "It goes to the next steps of the investigation, Your Honor."

Findlay just grinned at that. "Nice try, Mr. Brunelle, but no. This witness can't tell the jury what the expert said. You'll need to call the expert and have him tell the jury himself."

Fine with me, Brunelle thought. And now the jury knew it was important.

He shrugged. "Yes, Your Honor. Then I have no further questions for this witness at this time. We will recall the detective after Dr. Kieferman testifies."

Findlay frowned slightly. "That's your prerogative, counsel." He turned to the defense table. "Any cross-examination?"

Edwards stood up and shook her head. "I think I'll wait until he finishes later, Your Honor."

It was Findlay's turn to shrug. "Very well. You are excused, Detective Chen, but subject to recall." Then to Brunelle. "Call your next witness."

It was Carlisle who stood up. "The State calls Dr. Wilson Kieferman."

CHAPTER 35

Kieferman's testimony actually had to wait until the next day. They hadn't expected to be ready for him so soon and had already scheduled him for the next morning. That meant a slightly early adjournment for the day, which was fine by everyone. It was draining work to tell a story, even worse to listen to it.

So, the next morning, bright and early, the State called Dr. Wilson Kieferman to the stand.

Kieferman entered the courtroom abruptly, in the way only a large person can. He was very tall, with a large frame, and an outdated suit that he obviously hadn't worn since he was a little younger and a lot thinner. Generally, he didn't seem very kempt, or exceedingly clean, for that matter. His hair was sticking up in the back and his glasses were smudgy. He gave the impression of someone who didn't use mirrors regularly. But there was also a confidence that came from someone who didn't feel the need to use mirrors. He knew himself and he knew his stuff. And the jury was about to know it too.

"Please state your name for the record," Carlisle began.

"Wilson Emmanuel Kieferman," the witness answered, almost staccato.

"How are you employed, sir?"

"I am a forensic entomologist." There was obvious pride in Kieferman's voice.

"And what exactly is a forensic entomologist?" Carlisle followed up.

Kieferman sighed, and loudly. "It's exactly what it sounds like. I'm an entomologist, which means I study insects. I'm a forensic entomologist because I use my expertise in insects to analyze information and draw conclusions from real world situations."

"Like crimes?' Carlisle suggested.

"Yes." Kieferman sighed again. "Like crimes."

So much for having likeable witnesses, Brunelle thought.

"How long have you been a forensic entomologist?" Carlisle pressed ahead.

"I received my Ph.D. in entomology twenty-two years ago," Kieferman was obviously proud to report. "I have been doing forensic entomology for the last fifteen years. No, sixteen. Yes, sixteen years."

"You mentioned having a Ph.D.," Carlisle said. "So, did you obtain any special education or training to become a forensic entomologist?"

"Um, yes." Kieferman barely suppressed an eye roll. "B.S. in biology and biochemistry. M.S. in zoology and entomology. Ph.D. in entomology. Ongoing conferences as both an attendee and a lecturer. Do you want me to list every class I've attended or taught? That could take a while."

"No, thank you, that won't be necessary," Carlisle

assured him. "Have you ever worked with law enforcement to assist their investigations?"

"Yes," Kieferman lifted his chin a little as he responded. "All the time."

"All the time," Carlisle repeated. Brunelle wasn't sure if it was to reinforce Kieferman's credentials, or because it seemed unlikely the police would need a forensic entomologist all that often. "Okay. And did you consult with law enforcement regarding the case at issue here?"

"You mean the body behind the PetMax warehouse?" Kieferman confirmed. "Yes. Except I didn't *consult* with them. I examined the evidence and informed them of my conclusions."

Yep, definitely not likeable. Brunelle hoped he might come across as authoritative. In a good way.

"Okay," Carlisle accepted his answer. "Great. So, let's talk about those conclusions. But before we get into your specific findings as to this particular case, it might be helpful for the jury if we could step back and discuss generally what you were asked to do. What was it that the police were hoping you could shed some light on?"

"They wanted me to pinpoint a time of death," Kieferman explained. "Or at least a time at which the body was exposed to the elements, which would include local insect populations."

"Is that something you, as a forensic entomologist, are able to determine?" Carlisle asked.

"Uh, yes," Kieferman answered. His tone suggested he might add a 'duh' to the end of it, but fortunately he refrained.

"And how do you do that?" Carlisle asked. "Generally speaking?"

"Generally speaking," Kieferman mimicked, "flies like

rotting meat. Not to put too fine a point on it, but a dead body is rotting meat. That's why we put them six feet underground, so we don't have to watch and smell them rot. But flies love that smell. They're drawn to it. Flies will start landing on a dead body within minutes, especially if there's an open wound like in the case of a homicide."

"Like the case here?" Carlisle suggested.

"Right."

"So, again, generally speaking," Carlisle continued, "how are you, a forensic entomologist, able to determine a time of death, or of disposal, based on an examination of insects?"

Another sigh. "Okay, right." Kieferman seemed irritated to have to try to explain it to people without his expertise. "This is how it works. Dead body is exposed to elements. Flies smell the dead body. Flies land on the dead body. Flies lay eggs on the dead body. Eggs hatch on the dead body. Those are the maggots. Everybody knows dead bodies get maggots. What most people don't think about is that those maggots are fly larvae. They turn into adult flies. Then those adult flies lay eggs on the dead body. More eggs, more maggots, more flies. Lather, rinse, repeat. So, generally speaking, you can tell how long a dead body has been exposed to the elements based on the number of generations of flies and eggs and maggots present on the body, after taking into consideration a few variables."

"What variables?" Carlisle asked. Those were important. They were the weak point in his testimony.

Kieferman looked to the ceiling and rolled his wrist as he recited his list. "Local insect species, length of gestation and larval periods, ambient temperature, humidity, rainfall. But all of that can be determined. Species can be confirmed by examining a sample of adult flies found on the body. Weather conditions are recorded by outside agencies and can be consulted. So, if you know what you're doing, like I do, you have all the information you need to determine, to a very small window, an exact time of death."

"Or at least a time of being exposed to the elements," Carlisle hedged, "if we consider local fly populations to be part of the elements."

"I certainly do," Kieferman scoffed. "They're going to make much shorter work of a body than rain or wind or snow."

Carlisle nodded. "So, did you undertake that sort of examination in this case?"

"Yes, I did," Kieferman confirmed.

"Did you take samples of the flies and maggots?" Carlisle asked.

"Yes," Kieferman answered. "I was called out by the detective. Uh, Something Chang."

"Chen," Carlisle corrected. "Larry Chen."

"If you say so." Kieferman shrugged. "Anyway, I've done some other cases for Seattle P.D., so they called me again, and I went out to the scene before the body was collected by the medical examiner. There were a lot of insects, and they were definitely not going to transport all of them in the body bag to the morgue, so it was important I could do my work before they started doing theirs."

"So, what exactly did you do," Carlisle continued, "to try to determine the time the body had been disposed of?"

"I didn't try," Kieferman bristled. "I actually did it."

At least he was confident in his result, Brunelle considered. Hopefully the jury would be too.

"Okay," Carlisle absorbed the rebuke. "What did you do to actually determine the time the body had been disposed of?"

Kieferman counted off his steps on his fingers. "I took samples of adult and larval flies. I took photographs of the entire body and all of the infestations. I confirmed the species and their gestational and larval periods. I downloaded weather data from two different sources to confirm they matched each other—they did. I then used all of that information and my own expertise to determine the number of generations of flies living on that body and how long it would take for that many generations to happen, give or take 12-24 hours."

Brunelle didn't really like that last bit, but it wasn't too large a window, he supposed. It was still enough to focus in on the right day and get the license plate.

"And I should add," Kieferman continued, "the police use additional considerations to determine a more exact time of disposal. If I'm a murderer, I probably don't dump a body in broad daylight. So, I can tell the police it happened between, say two p.m. and two a.m. on such and such a date, but they will likely narrow it down to the hours of darkness, say six or seven p.m., reducing a twelve-hour window to only a six-hour window."

Carlisle didn't even need to ask. Nice.

"So, as you can see," Kieferman nodded at Carlisle, "I'm very helpful."

Carlisle managed a smile. "Of course you are. So, what was your conclusion in this case? How long had the body been exposed to the elements—including the local fly population—before it was discovered and examined by you?"

"Fifteen days prior to my examination," Kieferman answered, "between two p.m. and two a.m."

"So, the body was dumped between two p.m. and two a.m., fifteen days prior to your examination?" Carlisle repeated back to him.

"Yes." Kieferman frowned. "That's what I said."

Carlisle knew that, of course. They just wanted the jury to hear it twice.

Carlisle paused, as if trying to decide whether she needed to have Kieferman say anything else. He wasn't particularly enjoyable to listen to, and he'd given Carlisle what they needed. Brunelle looked at the jury. They seemed to share in that appraisal. They got it, but didn't seem to want any more of it. Carlisle agreed.

"No further questions, Your Honor," she announced.

Carlisle sat down and Edwards stood up. Again. Saxby was at the defense table, but he still hadn't done anything. Brunelle was starting to wonder if he ever would.

"So," Edwards sauntered up to the witness stand, "you can tell all that just by how many maggots are on the body?"

"I can," Kieferman answered. "Yes."

"And the variables are what again?"

"Species and weather," Kieferman summarized his earlier list.

"What about the extent of the injuries?" Edwards asked. "More injuries means more flies, right?"

"Not necessarily," Kieferman responded.

"Okay, but a person who just collapses from a heart attack is going to attract less flies than someone who has a large gaping wound, or several of them, right?" Edwards pressed him.

"Only at first," Kieferman said. "But decomposition begins immediately, and the flies will smell that long before any human would. There will be flies at the body's orifices within minutes."

"Still," Edwards wasn't ready to concede the point, "doesn't that change how long it would take to get to whatever amount of maggots you eventually use to try to calculate the time of death."

"I don't try to calculate," Kieferman said. "I do."

"Fine," Edwards sighed. "But answer my question. Couldn't that make a difference?"

"I take that into account," Kieferman said, not completely answering her question after all.

"How?" Edwards challenged. "What if you can't see the wound because of all the maggots? What if they've already eaten away all the flesh around the possible injury?"

"I take that into account," Kieferman repeated.

"But how?"

"I can tell whether there was an injury at the time of death based on the location of the colonies," Kieferman explained. "In this case, the insects were very significantly and very clearly concentrated around the neck and head. That indicates to me there was an injury there at the time of death. I believe that was later confirmed by the medical examiner."

"Who told you that?" Edwards demanded.

"Am I wrong?" Kieferman replied.

"That wasn't my question," Edwards raised her voice at him. "Did the prosecutor tell you what another witness is going to testify to?"

"No, ma'am," Kieferman replied calmly. "I care about my work. That means following up to confirm I was right. I contacted the Medical Examiner's Office myself to see if I was right. And, as I expected, I was right."

Edwards frowned. Brunelle breathed a sigh of relief. Juries don't like it when prosecutors don't play fair. Edwards thought she'd caught him. Luckily, he knew better than to coach his witnesses.

"So, there's no variability at all?" Edwards complained. "Just species and weather? And even then, you can't pinpoint it but to a twelve-hour window."

"That's very specific," Kieferman defended.

"It is. I agree," Edwards said. "But if there was something off in your data—"

"There wasn't," Kieferman cut her off.

Edwards sighed again. "Ok. Let me ask it a different way. How far would the data have to vary to impact your estimate by say another twelve hours? Like the temperature. One degree? Two degrees?"

"No." Kieferman shook his head. "That's not enough.

"Five degrees?"

Kieferman considered for a moment. "Five degrees might be enough to change my determination. Maybe even four degrees."

"Okay, now we're getting somewhere," Edwards said. "What about humidity, or rainfall, or whatever else you said about the weather?"

"It really depends," Kieferman insisted. "All of these variables interact with each other. You'd need a Ph.D. to understand it all. I have that Ph.D."

"And I don't," Edwards pointed out. "Is that what you're saying?"

"You said it," Kieferman didn't disagree. "Not me."

"So, we're just supposed to take your word for it?" Edwards asked.

Kieferman thought for a few moments, then smiled at Edwards. "Yes."

Kieferman was definitely a jerk. But he was the prosecution's jerk. Edwards decided to give it up.

"No further questions, Your Honor," she conceded and walked back toward the defense table.

"Any redirect examination?" Judge Findlay asked Carlisle.

Carlisle stood up and nodded. "Just briefly, Your Honor. Thank you." She turned to Kieferman, but asked her questions from behind the prosecution table.

"To be clear, it wasn't five degrees warmer, was it?"

"No," Kieferman answered. "It was the temperature it was."

"And the fly species was the fly species," Carlisle said, "and the rainfall was the rainfall, right?"

"Right," Kieferman confirmed.

"And based on the actual data, you estimated—" She corrected herself. "I'm sorry, you *determined* the time the body was disposed of was fifteen days prior to the discovery, between two a.m. and two p.m., correct?"

It didn't hurt for the jury to hear it a third time.

"Correct."

"No further questions."

Rather than ask Edwards whether she had any re-cross-examination, Judge Findlay suggested his preferred answer by asking her, "May this witness be excused?"

Edwards acquiesced. "Yes, Your Honor."

Kieferman pushed his large frame out of the witness chair and looked around for someone to give him further direction, or a handshake, or something. But he had to just lumber out of the courtroom on his own. The lawyers were already thinking about the next witness.

It made sense to recall Chen then to talk about getting the security video. That had been the original plan. But Brunelle didn't like how Edwards had made the investigation sound in her opening. She wasn't wrong, but it made the discovery of Stephanie Pang sound like the last second act of desperation it was. They needed it to sound better than that.

Chronological was best, except when it wasn't. The jury would naturally assume the information they received was chronological. It was almost subconscious. That meant Brunelle could bolster his case by making it feel like the identification of Kincaid as the killer happened, not right after one body had been discovered, but rather after both bodies were discovered.

The next witness wouldn't be Chen. It would be the officer who arrested Brunelle.

CHAPTER 36

This would be another Carlisle witness, if only because it would have been awkward for Brunelle to question the man who'd shoved him face down in mud and handcuffed him only a few weeks earlier. Officer William Redding of the Seattle Police Department.

"Please state your name," Carlisle began.

"Bill Redding, ma'am," he answered. He was young, a new cop, recently out of the military, still sporting the haircut and posture. That was fine. So, he was a little formal. It could have been worse.

"How are you employed?"

"I am a police officer with the Seattle Police Department, ma'am."

"How long have you been a police officer?" Carlisle continued.

"Two years next month, ma'am."

Brunelle wondered if every single answer was going to end with 'ma'am'. He didn't recall any sirs when Redding was wrenching his arms behind his back.

"What are your current duties and assignments?"

"Patrol," Redding answered. "I respond to calls and look for crimes in progress."

Okay, that was the preliminary stuff. Time to get to the details.

"Were you involved in the discovery of a body in the area of West Marginal Way, south of the old PetMax warehouse?"

Redding thought for a moment. "I'm not familiar with that particular business, ma'am. It may have closed before I started. But I was definitely involved in the recovery of some human remains on West Marginal Way in White Center. That's not something you would forget."

Carlisle nodded. So did a couple of the jurors. "Okay, just very generally, how did you become involved?"

Redding turned to the jurors to give his answer. He was new, but the class about testifying was at the academy before they were even commissioned. "At approximately twenty hundred hours, we got a call about a possible trespasser behind one of the closed businesses down there. I forget which one right now, but it was fenced off with some of that temporary chain-link fence. I self-dispatched along with Officer Lopez. When we arrived, we observed a vehicle. It was empty, but it was still running, and its headlights were on, pointing into the woods behind the business. We searched the area and located a white male behind the business."

"And what did you do with this white male?" Carlisle seemed a little too happy to ask.

"We drew our weapons and detained him."

Shoved him into the mud and handcuffed him is more like it,

Brunelle thought ruefully. But he kept a pleasant expression on his face.

"Did the man identify himself?" Carlisle asked.

"Yes, ma'am," Redding confirmed. "He said he was a homicide prosecutor with the King County Prosecutor's Office."

Carlisle turned around and pointed at Brunelle. "Is that the man you detained that night?"

Redding took a moment to size up Brunelle. "Yes, ma'am. That's him."

"Did he say what he was doing there?"

"He said he was looking into a report of a missing person," Redding recounted, "and had run across possible human remains."

"And were there, in fact, human remains located there?"

"Yes, ma'am. A skeleton anyway."

"Did you do anything with those remains?" Carlisle followed up.

"No, ma'am," Redding answered. "I'm just a patrol officer. I can detain a trespasser, but I know not to touch human remains. I called for homicide to respond, then locked down the scene while Officer Lopez dealt with the gentleman over there." A nod toward Brunelle.

"Did a homicide detective arrive?" Carlisle asked.

"Yes, ma'am."

"Who?"

"It was Detective Chen. I don't know his first name," Redding apologized. "Like I said, I'm just patrol."

"And Detective Chen took over the investigation?"

"Yes, ma'am."

"Thank you, Officer Redding," Carlisle concluded. "No further questions."

Edwards stood up as Carlisle sat down. Brunelle was just trying not to look mortified. He was fully expecting Edwards to try to embarrass him.

"So, you weren't involved in the collection of the remains of the body?" Edwards began.

"Not directly, ma'am," Redding answered. "I maintained scene security while the detectives and the folks from the Medical Examiner took care of that."

"Did you disturb the body in any way?" Edwards asked.

"Me?" clarified Redding in a way that invited exactly the follow-up question Brunelle was dreading. "No, not me."

"What about him?" Edwards pointed at Brunelle.

Redding nodded. "He might have stepped on it. Or in it, I suppose. It was pretty far gone."

Edwards grinned. Not at the state of the remains, just at the thought of Brunelle literally stepping in it. "No further questions."

"Any redirect examination?" Findlay asked Carlisle.

"About me stepping in a dead body?" Brunelle hissed at her. "No fucking way."

Carlisle stood up. "Apparently not, Your Honor. Thank you."

CHAPTER 37

There was still a bit more to do before they could recall Chen. Brunelle wanted the whole story of both bodies told before Chen returned to explain how they identified Kincaid and linked him to the murders. They called all of the other officers involved in the collection and documentation of the two bodies. That may not have been the exact order of events in the real world, but he could make it the order of events inside the courtroom. Two murders, same location, same manner of death. Then, license plate for Ashleigh and blood stain for Stephanie. Too much to be a coincidence. Rest and convict. That was the plan.

Best laid plans… Brunelle couldn't help but think. He wasn't wrong, but he was a little premature.

The last witness before Chen retook the stand was the medical examiner who had conducted the autopsies of both Ashleigh Engel and Stephanie Pang. The jury needed to hear that they had died the same way, and since neither of them had any flesh left where the fatal injuries had been delivered, photos weren't going to tell the story. That meant someone else had to.

"Dr. Elissa Welbourne," was that someone else, as she answered the usual first question. She was a fifty-something African American woman, with short hair and small glasses. She looked like a high school science teacher, the one you remembered fondly years later.

"How are you employed?" Carlisle asked. It was her turn again, in part because Brunelle would be going next. Then Carlisle would finish with the DNA expert from the crime lab. It was always good to end big and, short of a confession they didn't have anyway, there wasn't much bigger than a DNA match.

"I'm an assistant medical examiner with the King County Medical Examiner's Office," Welbourne answered.

Next, she explained her education and experience. B.S. M.D. Residency in forensic pathology. Internship with the Fresno County Medical Examiner's Office in California. Ongoing training and courses since arriving at the King County M.E.'s Office five years ago.

"Do your current duties include performing autopsies?" Carlisle continued.

"That's a significant part of my current duties, yes," Welbourne confirmed.

"Approximately how many autopsies have you conducted in your career?"

Welbourne took a moment to think. "Gosh, well over three thousand, I would estimate."

"That's a lot," Carlisle observed.

"It sure is," Welbourne acknowledged.

"Are all of them suspected homicides?"

"Oh, no," Welbourne assured. "Homicides are actually a

small proportion of the autopsies we perform. We do autopsies any time cause of death is uncertain. Drug overdoses, exposure, suicide. Similarly, we don't do them when the cause of death is obvious or expected, for example, a heart attack or cancer. Hospitals may do their own limited forensic examinations to confirm an expected cause of death, but the County Medical Examiner's Office only gets involved if there's a State interest in determining cause and manner of death."

"Like homicide?" Carlisle suggested.

"Like homicide," Welbourne agreed.

"Okay, now, before we talk about your specific findings in this case," Carlisle moved along, "it might be helpful if you could explain to the jury the difference between manner of death and cause of death?"

"Sure," Welbourne answered. She turned to the jury. "There are four manners of death: homicide, suicide, accident, and natural causes. Cause of death means the specific mechanism that caused the death, for example, like gunshot wound, blunt force trauma, asphyxiation, et cetera. So, a gunshot wound can be the cause of death for a homicide, but also for a suicide or even for an accident."

"Thank you," Carlisle accepted the answer and moved forward. "Did you have occasions to conduct the autopsies on Ashleigh Engel and Stephanie Pang, the alleged victims in this case?"

"I did," Welbourne confirmed.

"And were you able to determine the manner and cause of death for both of those individuals?"

"I was."

"Regarding Ashleigh Engel," Carlisle asked first, "what were the manner and cause of death?"

"The cause of death for Ashleigh Engel was a single gunshot wound to the left side of the skull," Welbourne answered. "The manner of death was homicide."

"And regarding Stephanie Pang," Carlisle asked next, "what were the manner and cause of death?"

"The same," Welbourne said. "The cause of death was a single gunshot wound to the left side of the skull. The manner of death was homicide."

Brunelle relaxed a bit. That was the major part of the doctor's testimony they needed to elicit, and it had come out clean and clear, with no distracting objections. But they weren't quite done.

"Were there any challenges," Carlisle asked, "posed by the condition of the remains when you went to examine them?"

"Oh, yes," Welbourne confirmed. "Definitely."

"What were those?"

"Well, with Ms. Engel, the biggest challenge was the insect infestation," Welbourne answered. "It's my understanding the police cleared off a lot of them, but there were quite a few that were deeper in the tissue and therefore made the transport to my office. So, we had to deal with that first. A related challenge was that the maggots had left very little soft tissue on the head and shoulders."

"What about with regard to Ms. Pang?" Carlisle asked.

"It was a similar challenge," Welbourne responded. "Those remains were basically just a skeleton. So, in both instances, I could only examine the skull to determine the cause of death. There was no soft tissue to help decipher what had happened."

"Why did that present a challenge?" Carlisle asked.

"Well, with gunshot wounds, like in these cases,"

Welbourne explained, "the bullet travels through the soft tissue before striking bone. If that's gone, we can't always determine the trajectory. Imagine a shot through the stomach that only hits soft tissue, no bones. If the flesh is gone, there would be no evidence of the path."

"But here, there was some evidence of the bullet trajectory, correct?" Carlisle knew to clarify.

"Yes," Welbourne confirmed, "because the bullet penetrated the skull, damaging it. So, I could at least examine that."

"And did you?"

"Yes, of course."

"And what were you able to determine from those examinations?" Carlisle prompted.

"Each skull suffered a single entrance wound."

"How do you know it was an entrance wound?"

"Well, for one thing, there was no second hole," Welbourne answered. "So, unless the gun was inside the victim's skull cavity—which I highly doubt—one hole means entrance. For a second thing, it's very common for a bullet to penetrate the skull on one side but not be able to exit on the other side. Bullets lose velocity after going through something as thick as a skull. Rather than exit the other side, the bullet will ricochet inside, and there were marks on the interior of the skull consistent with ricochets like that. For a third thing, the hole was round and beveled, which is what happens on the side where a bullet enters. Exit wounds are characterized by irregular tears and breaks where the bullet breaks through. Finally, and this was the real clue, I located a spent round inside one of the skulls."

"Which skull?" Carlisle asked.

"Ashleigh Engel's skull," Welbourne answered. The body with the insects."

"But you didn't find a bullet inside Stephanie Pang's skull?" Carlisle inquired.

"No," Welbourne confirmed. "That was just a skeleton. The bullet was likely lost prior to discovery due to things like rain or wild animals. Once the soft tissue was completely gone, the spent round could have rolled out of the skull quite easily."

Carlisle frowned, but nodded. "So, we can't compare the bullets to see if they were fired from the same gun?"

"I don't believe so. Not without the bullets," Welbourne answered. "But I can say the bullets were the same caliber. I measured the holes, and they were exactly the same diameter."

That was something, Brunelle supposed.

"One more thing," Carlisle said. "Were you able to tell how far away the gun was when either victim was shot?"

Welbourne shook her head. "No, not without soft tissue. If there had still been skin near the gunshot wound, I could have examined for signs of burning or stippling from heat and bits of hot gunpowder exiting the barrel after the bullet, but there was nothing to examine in these cases. A bullet will make the same size hole in bone whether it's one inch away or one hundred yards away."

Carlisle nodded for a moment, then wrapped up. "So, to summarize, both Ashleigh Engel and Stephanie Pang died from a single gunshot wound to the head, at the same approximate location on the skull, with the same caliber bullet. Is that all correct?"

"Yes," Welbourne confirmed. "That's all correct."

"Thank you. No further questions." And Carlisle returned to her seat.

Edwards stood up again. Saxby had done nothing but sit on the other side of Kincaid the entire trial. Maybe he could run out and get everyone coffee.

"You said the bullet from Stephanie Pang's skull could be missing because of rain or animals?" Edwards asked.

"That's correct," Welbourne answered. "Once the soft tissue is gone, there are several openings through which the bullet could have fallen."

"What about someone accidentally tripping over and stepping on the remains?" Edwards asked, with a side glance at Brunelle. "That could have sent the bullet rolling out of the skull and into the mud, right?"

"Sure," Welbourne agreed. "I suppose so. Anything that jostled the skull."

Edwards grinned. "No further questions."

And fuck you too, thought Brunelle, decidedly without any grin.

Carlisle didn't have any redirect exam. It was finally time to recall Chen.

CHAPTER 38

When last the jury had heard from the calm, almost stoic, Detective Larry Chen, he was about to tell them what he had done after the Bug Guy told him how long Ashleigh Engel's body had been out behind the PetMax warehouse when it was discovered by Ginger the Doberman Pinscher—before being so rudely, albeit justifiably, interrupted by a legitimate objection from the defense, or rather, from Edwards, since Saxby was still doing his impression of a potted plant.

Brunelle picked up right where they left off.

"Was Dr. Kieferman able to tell you how long Ashleigh Engel's body had been out in the elements before it was finally located by law enforcement?"

"Yes, he was," Chen answered.

"And what did he tell you?"

Chen paused for a moment to see if Edwards might object again, but no objection was forthcoming. "Fifteen days, between fourteen-hundred hours and zero-two-hundred hours."

"So, between two p.m. to two a.m.?" Brunelle translated.

"Correct." Chen gave a contrite nod to the civilian jurors. "Sorry about that."

"So, armed with that information," Brunelle continued, "what did you do next?"

"Well, as I said, I wanted witnesses," Chen reminded the jurors. "But to find those I needed to find out who might have been nearby when the body was disposed of. Once the insect expert gave me a twelve-hour window, I was able to look into whether there might have been anyone who saw anything suspicious or noteworthy during that relatively short time period."

"Were you able to locate anyone who saw anything suspicious or noteworthy?" Brunelle asked.

"Any person? No," Chen answered. "But sometimes the best witnesses are cameras."

Brunelle nodded, and noticed at least one other juror join him. "Did a camera pick up something suspicious or noteworthy during the time period identified by Dr. Kieferman?"

"Yes," Chen told the jurors, "and something useful."

"Please explain," Brunelle invited.

So Chen did. "All of the buildings there were abandoned except for Delaney and Sons. That meant there were no workers at any of the buildings except Delaney and Sons. It turns out Mr. Unger was working the night the body was dumped, too. He didn't recall seeing anything, but he was able to access the security cameras for us. The business had a lot of cameras. More than a dozen. Most were pointing at the back lot, but there were also ones over every entrance. One was pointing at the south parking lot, which just so happened to be between Delaney and Sons and PetMax."

"And that camera picked up something?" Brunelle interjected.

"Yes."

Brunelle stepped over to the exhibit counter and retrieved a CD in a paper sleeve. He handed it to Chen.

"Detective, I'm now handing you what is marked as Exhibit Number Three," Brunelle said for the record. "Do you recognize this?"

Chen took the exhibit. "Yes."

"Generally speaking, what is it?" Brunelle asked.

"It's a compact disc," Chen identified.

"Does it appear to be related to this case?"

"Yes, it does."

"And how do you know that?" Brunelle asked.

"It has the case name and case number written on it," Chen explained, "and it's in my handwriting. I made this CD."

"And what's on the CD?"

"It's a copy of the video we reviewed in this case," Chen told the jury.

Brunelle then moved to admit the exhibit. Edwards didn't object. Next, he moved to publish it—that is, play it for the jury. Again, no objection from Edwards. In fact, she seemed almost disinterested in it.

What followed next was the awkward dance of pulling down the screen on the far wall, connecting the laptop to the courtroom projector, queuing up the file on the CD, and dimming the lights, all while trying not to look like a middle-aged lawyer who graduated law school before 'tech' was even a job field—let alone the one that took over your hometown.

"Okay, I think I got it," Brunelle announced after a few minutes. "So, Detective, I'm going to press play and if you could just sort of narrate along and tell us what we're seeing. Okay?"

Chen had done this type of testimony before. He'd done every type of testimony before. "Okay."

The video quality wasn't great, and it was pretty dark, but with the courtroom lights dimmed, it was possible to make out at least some of the shapes on the screen. It was good Chen was telling everyone what they were seeing.

"So, you can see the time stamp in the corner says zero-twenty-nine hours, twelve-twenty-nine a.m.," Chen began his narration. "Now, you can see a vehicle entering the parking lot, approaching from the south on West Marginal. Once it's in the parking lot, you can see it turns off its headlights and rolls to the back of the lot. There aren't any lights on the warehouse, just streetlights up on West Marginal, so when the car rolls behind the warehouse, you really can't see anything. Now, nothing happens for a while—nothing that can be seen by the camera anyway. Then, after approximately four minutes, you can see the vehicle comes back out from behind the warehouse, again with its headlights off. As it reaches West Marginal, the headlights come on again and the vehicle turns north, driving past the front of Delaney and Sons."

That was the end of the clip.

"Were you able to get a license plate from the video?" Brunelle asked.

"Not from that camera," Chen explained, "but we synced up the time stamps with the cameras on the front of the business, facing the road, and we were able to observe the same vehicle drive past. Using still frames from those cameras, we zoomed in and determined the license plate."

Brunelle walked to the exhibit counter and picked up two photographs.

"Detective, I'm now handing you what have been marked as Exhibits Four and Five," Brunelle said, again for the record, as he handed the photographs to Chen. "Generally speaking, what types of documents are these?"

"These are photographs," Chen answered, also for the record, and a bit for the jury.

"And what do they appear to be photographs of?"

"They are photographs of a vehicle license plate," Chen answered.

"Are you familiar with how these photographs were obtained?"

"Yes. These are blowups from still frames of the video we just watched," Chen explained.

"So, this is the license plate of the vehicle we just observed driving to the back of the PetMax warehouse, with its headlights dimmed, at the exact time Dr. Kieferman determined the body was dumped there?" Brunelle spelled it out for the jury.

"Yes," Chen answered.

"The State moves to admit Exhibits Four and Five," Brunelle addressed his request to the judge.

"Any objection, Ms. Edwards?" Findlay asked, as was customary on any motion to admit evidence.

Edwards stood up to reply. "To the photos? No, no objection."

Brunelle frowned inside. That 'to the photos?' meant she had something else she was preparing to object to.

"Exhibits Four and Five are admitted," Judge Findlay ruled.

Brunelle next took a several-page, stapled document off the counter. "Detective, I'm now handing you what's been marked as Exhibit Six. What type of document is this?"

"This is a certified copy of a vehicle registration," Chen told the jurors. "It tells us who the registered owner is for a given license plate."

"And does it appear to be the vehicle registration for the license plate photographed in Exhibits Four and Five?"

"It does, yes," Chen confirmed.

Brunelle just needed to have the exhibit admitted and then Chen would be allowed to read the registered owner's name to the jury. It was a bit of a formality—everyone in the courtroom knew Kincaid was the registered owner, or Brunelle wouldn't be asking—but trials were all about formality.

"The State moves to admit Exhibit Six," Brunelle told Judge Findlay.

Again, Findlay asked Edwards, "Any objection?"

Edwards stood up again. "Actually, yes, Your Honor. The defense objects."

Brunelle didn't roll his eyes in front of the jury, but internally, they were way back in his skull.

"What's the basis of the objection?" Findlay asked for him.

"Lack of foundation," Edwards answered. "Those photographs are very low quality, Your Honor. They are blown up from stills of a video of a car speeding past at night. I don't believe they show the license plate with sufficient clarity to connect it to the vehicle registration Mr. Brunelle is seeking to admit."

Brunelle picked the photographs up and looked at them. They weren't perfect, but you could definitely make out the numbers and letters. At least Brunelle thought so.

"May   I   examine   the   witness   regarding   the

photographs?" Edwards requested.

Findlay could allow it. If Edwards could establish that the photos didn't actually connect to the vehicle registration, then Findlay could—and should—deny the motion to admit. But Brunelle doubted Chen would torpedo his case by agreeing with Edwards.

"Proceed," Findlay agreed to Edwards's request.

Brunelle stepped back as Edwards came out from behind her counsel table and approached Chen. She picked up the photographs herself and set them out in front of Chen at the witness stand.

She pointed at one of the digits pictured. "Is that a B or an eight?"

"It's a B," Chen answered.

"Are you sure?"

Chen took a moment to look at the photo. "Yes, I'm sure."

"What about that?" Edwards pointed to another symbol. "Is that a K or an H?"

"It's a K," Chen answered without hesitation.

"Really?" Edwards squinted at the photo. "It kind of looks like an H to me."

"It's a K, counselor," Chen said. Then added, "And before you ask, I can tell you that last letter is an A, not a four."

Edwards smiled at that. "Well, then. Thank you, Detective."

She started to walk away, then turned back. "But you would agree with me, if that B was really an eight, or that K was really an H, or that A was a four, then that wouldn't be my client's license plate, would it?"

"If," Chen repeated the key word. "But they aren't. It's

his plate."

Edwards smiled again and nodded. "If you say so, Detective."

She returned to her seat, then looked up at the judge. "We maintain our objection for the record, Your Honor."

But she and Brunelle both knew Findlay would overrule it. Which he promptly did. "Exhibit Six is admitted."

"Please read the name of the registered owner for that license plate, Detective Chen," Brunelle instructed as he came back out from behind his table.

Chen nodded, then turned to the jury. "The registered owner is Michael James Kincaid."

That had the desired effect. A little anticlimactic after Edwards's objection, but still, they had just linked Kincaid to the Ashleigh Engel murder. Now to connect him to Stephanie Pang.

Brunelle stepped over to the exhibit counter and picked up the search warrant for Kincaid's car. "Did you eventually locate that vehicle and conduct a search?"

But before Chen could answer, Edwards jumped to her feet. "Your Honor!" she called out. "I have a motion."

CHAPTER 39

Brunelle tried to keep the feeling of '*Oh, shit*' off of his expression, but it filled his mind and gut. He didn't know what Edwards's motion was, which made it even worse. Good lawyers could anticipate each other's moves, but Brunelle was in the dark. All he knew was, Edwards was a good lawyer, and she'd waited until the exact right moment to interrupt his case.

"I'm not sure what the motion is, Your Honor," Brunelle tried, "but I'd like to proceed with this current line of questioning before we address it."

Of course, he would. Whatever Edwards's motion was, it was intended exactly to stop his current line of questioning. Brunelle knew that. So did Edwards. And so did Findlay.

He turned to the jurors. "Ladies and gentlemen, I'm going to ask you to retire to the jury room. Sometimes legal issues arise which need to be argued and decided outside of the presence of the jury. I'm hopeful this interruption won't take very long."

The jurors shrugged at each other, then stood up and made their way out of the courtroom, led by the bailiff who had risen to escort them to the jury room. When the door closed behind them, Judge Findlay looked down at Edwards.

"What's your motion, counsel?"

"It's a motion to suppress, Your Honor," Edwards answered. "I'm moving to suppress any evidence obtained from the search of my client's vehicle which is related to the investigation of the murder of Stephanie Pang."

"Only that evidence?" Findlay asked. "Not the entire search?"

"No, Your Honor," Edwards confirmed. "Just the information regarding Stephanie Pang."

Findlay frowned a bit at the request, then turned to Brunelle. "Any response?"

Brunelle looked around for a moment. The Pangs, seated in the front row like every other day of the trial, looked worried. Carlisle looked suspicious. Edwards looked pleased with herself. Brunelle supposed he looked confused, which he went with since the jury wasn't there to see it anyway.

"I'm not sure how to respond, Your Honor," Brunelle admitted. "I understand what Ms. Edwards is asking for, but I haven't heard any legal basis to support it."

Findlay turned back to the defense table. "Ms. Edwards, care to educate Mr. Brunelle and myself regarding the basis of your motion?"

"May I approach the witness, Your Honor?" Edwards asked. She was enjoying the show. She looked too confident. Brunelle felt his confidence waning in the glow of hers.

Findlay hesitated, but then sighed and gestured toward Chen, who was still sitting on the witness stand. "Proceed."

"Thank you, Your Honor." Edwards bowed her head slightly to the judge, then stepped forward and picked up the search warrant documents. She handed one to Chen. "Is this the affidavit you executed to obtain the search warrant for my client's vehicle?"

Chen took his time examining the papers before answering. He didn't know what Edwards was doing either, but he knew enough not to trust her. "It appears to be."

Edwards just smiled at that hedge. "Okay, and is that your signature on the last page of the affidavit?"

Chen flipped to the last page. "Yes," he acknowledged.

"Great, great," Edwards said. "And this is the only affidavit for search warrant on my client's vehicle, correct? You only searched it the one time, correct? You didn't go back again after Ms. Pang's remains were found, right?"

Chen nodded slowly. "Right."

"Fantastic," Edwards replied. "Okay, could you just go ahead and look at the first page of the warrant, where you list out the items you were searching for?"

Chen turned back to the first page. "Right here?"

"Yes, right there," Edwards confirmed. "Just go ahead and read that list of potential evidence to the Court."

Chen looked at Brunelle for a moment, but he couldn't offer more than a shrug. He was curious to find out what Edwards's point was. Curious, and a little afraid.

Chen picked up mid-sentence, "To then and there search for the following items of evidence: any evidence related to the murder of Ashleigh Engel, to include weapons, clothing, bodily fluids, trace evidence, DNA evidence, paper documents, and other items reasonably related to the investigation."

"And did you find any weapons, clothing, bodily fluids, trace evidence, DNA evidence, paper documents, or other items reasonably related to the investigation of the murder of

Ashleigh Engel?"

Chen hesitated. Brunelle finally understood. His heart almost stopped. They hadn't known about Stephanie Pang—or any of Kincaid's other victims—when Chen wrote the affidavit for warrant.

"Uh..."Chen started. "Not exactly, but—"

"Did you find any weapons that could be linked to the murder of Ashleigh Engel?" Edwards interrupted.

"Um, no," Chen had to admit.

"Did you find any clothing that could be linked to the murder of Ashleigh Engel?" Edwards continued.

"No," Chen answered.

"Did you find any bodily fluids, trace evidence, or DNA evidence connected to the murder of Ashleigh Engel?"

Chen shifted in his seat. "Not directly, but—"

"Not directly," Edwards repeated. "Not at all, correct?"

Chen wasn't sure how to answer.

"Did you find Ashleigh Engel's DNA anywhere in my client's car?" Edwards demanded.

"No, ma'am," Chen conceded.

"In fact, the only thing you found of any value," Edwards pressed, "related not to the murder of Ashleigh Engel, but to the murder of Stephanie Pang. Isn't that true, Detective Chen?"

"We collected DNA from the trunk of your client's car," Chen explained, "that was later determined to be from Stephanie Pang."

"Later determined," Edwards echoed. "After the search, correct?"

"Yes, ma'am."

"The search that was only authorized to collect evidence

regarding the murder of Ashleigh Engel, correct?" Edwards demanded.

"That's one way of looking at it," Chen answered.

"It sure is," Edwards agreed. "No further questions, Your Honor."

Findlay raised an eyebrow at Brunelle. "Any questions for the witness based on those questions, Mr. Brunelle?"

There was no point. Chen had told the truth. There wasn't anything to add. "No, Your Honor. I'm prepared for argument."

Judge Findlay nodded. "This is your motion, Ms. Edwards. You go first, although I think we all know what your argument is."

Edwards gave another respectful nod to the judge. "I'm sure we all do, Your Honor," she said. "And that's because it's obviously correct. The Fourth Amendment to the United States Constitution and Article One, Section Seven, of the Washington State Constitution both prohibit unreasonable searches and seizures. A warrantless search is per se unreasonable. Search warrants must be limited in scope and duration, and only authorize the collection of evidence specifically enumerated in the affidavit for search warrant. If, during a lawful search for one type of evidence, police encounter evidence of a different crime, they must stop the search and seek an additional warrant for the newly discovered evidence. This is the settled, black letter law on searches. Nothing there is new."

Brunelle could hardly argue with that.

"Here," Edwards continued, "the search warrant only authorized what the detective asked for: evidence related to the murder of Ashleigh Engel. It did not authorize the collection of evidence related to the murder of anyone else, and certainly not

Stephanie Pang. Therefore, any evidence collected related to the murder of Stephanie Pang was obtained outside of the warrant and without lawful authority. Evidence obtained from a search conducted without lawful authority must be suppressed from evidence at trial. Accordingly, any evidence regarding the murder of Stephanie Pang must be suppressed.

"If the prosecutor wants the witness to tell the jury that they found nothing in my client's car related to the murder of Ashleigh Engel, I will not object. But I do object to any evidence regarding Stephanie Pang, and I would ask the Court to suppress any such evidence. Thank you."

Brunelle watched Findlay's face for any sign of his opinion of Edwards's argument, but the judge's expression was inscrutable. He turned, poker faced, to Brunelle. "Response?"

Brunelle looked to Carlisle to see if she wanted perhaps to address Edwards's arguments, but she shook her head at him. "Your witness, man."

Brunelle sighed and looked back at the judge. "Thank you, Your Honor. I will concede that Ms. Edwards's argument has a certain superficial appeal. But it relies too heavily on law and avoids the actual facts of these cases. In particular, it ignores completely the way these two cases are intertwined, a fact which the Court recognized when Your Honor denied Ms. Edwards's motion to sever."

That was a risky thing to bring up, Brunelle knew. Findlay was probably ruing his ruling just then. If he had severed the cases for trial, Edwards's motion would be far less important; she might not have raised it at all.

"I could go on about how detectives are not required to ignore evidence of a crime when conducting a search," Brunelle continued. "I could explain that a second warrant would not have made sense since the DNA in question had already been collected and removed during the first search. But, instead, I would argue that the DNA of Stephanie Pang in the defendant's trunk *is* evidence related to the murder of Ashleigh Engel."

Findlay's eyebrow raised even higher at that assertion. Brunelle decided to take it as encouragement rather than incredulity. Although, really, he knew better.

"As we explained at the hearing on the motion to sever," Brunelle went on, the "evidence of these two crimes is interrelated. The similarity of the victims, the proximity of the dump sites, the identical method of death. Each provides evidence and context to the other. The fact that the DNA of a woman dumped less than a quarter of a mile from Ashleigh Engel's body was found inside the vehicle observed driving away from Ashleigh Engel's body is, in fact, evidence 'related to' the murder of Ashleigh Engel. The warrant says, 'related to'. It doesn't say, 'exclusively related to' or 'only related to'. The language is intentionally broad. The evidence found during that search is inextricably related to the murder of both women, and as such, falls within the plain language of the warrant. Ms. Edwards's argument is creative, but it's too clever for its own good, and the Court should deny it. Thank you."

Brunelle sat down again. He was hoping for a 'Good job' from Carlisle, but her gaze was fixed on Findlay. What he said next could alter the outcome of the cases, both of them.

Findlay seemed fully aware of that fact himself. Brunelle felt a pang of regret at having won the motion on severance. Judges hated ruling on the close calls, the ones that really could go either way. That motion for severance had been one of those. This new motion to suppress because of the language of the warrant was another. Close calls were hard because the arguments might fall 51% to 49%, but the winner walked away with 100%. One way to even that out—and one that a lot of judges employed, to the consternation of the lawyers who appeared before them—was to offset the award of a close call to one side with the award of the next close call to the other side. Tit for tat, or something like that. If Findlay did that—and he might if he was deeply regretting not having severed the cases for trial—Brunelle was in trouble.

And Brunelle was indeed in trouble.

"I appreciate Mr. Brunelle's creative advocacy," Findlay began, throwing Brunelle's own backhanded compliment back at him, "but I do not believe the intent of Detective Chen when he filled out the affidavit for search warrant, or of the judge who signed that search warrant in response to the affidavit, was to collect evidence of other crimes with the hope of later linking them back to the murder of Ashleigh Engel through proximity in time or place. The plain language of the warrant is for evidence related to the murder of Ashleigh Engel, nothing more. DNA of a different victim is undeniably more, and was never authorized by the judge, nor sought to be authorized by the detective. That only makes sense, as they were unaware of the second crime, but it doesn't change the legal infirmity of the warrant. The warrant was evidence related to the murder of Ashleigh Engel, and I will allow testimony as to any such evidence, although it sounds like from the arguments that no such evidence exists. But I will grant Ms. Edwards's motion and suppress any mention of evidence collected from that vehicle related to any other crimes, including the murder of Stephanie Pang."

Brunelle couldn't believe it. "Your Honor…" he tried.

"I've made my ruling, counsel," Findlay snapped at him.

"I won't hear any further argument. Are you ready to proceed with your witness?"

Brunelle blinked a few times and shook his head. He turned and looked at Carlisle, intentionally avoiding the astonished gaze of the Pangs in the front row. Carlisle just shrugged. "Your witness, Dave."

Brunelle nodded, shell shocked. "Sure, Your Honor," he finally replied. "Why not?"

Findlay nodded to his bailiff, who jumped up again and hurried to the jury room door to bring the jurors back into the courtroom. When they retook their seats, Findlay didn't tell them what the motion had been or how he had ruled. He just nodded to Brunelle and said, "Next question, counsel."

But there were no more questions. Chen had linked Kincaid to Engel through the surveillance video and vehicle registration. And Chen wouldn't be allowed to connect Kincaid to Pang through the DNA evidence. Brunelle wanted to recover, to plow ahead confidently so the jury wouldn't suspect how badly Findlay had just kneecapped him, but he had nothing. Nothing at all.

"No further questions, Your Honor," he said weakly, then turned to sit down again.

"Cross-examination?" Findlay invited Edwards to question Chen. Normally, a defense attorney could spend hours cross-examining the lead detective, but she had just done more damage than she ever could have done through cross. And if she didn't ask any questions, Brunelle couldn't ask any more either. She could just leave it where it was and point out the complete lack of evidence in the Pang case in her closing argument.

She stood up confidently. "No questions, Your Honor."

That was the smartest play.

Chen was excused, and Findlay practically glowered down at the prosecution table. "Does the State have any further witnesses?"

The answer was no. Not now. No need for the DNA expert when the DNA wasn't admissible. But Brunelle was thinking just clearly enough to know he wasn't capable of thinking clearly just then.

"The State would ask to adjourn until tomorrow morning, Your Honor," he requested. "We will put on further witnesses then, if any."

'If any'. Findlay knew what that meant. He showed Brunelle the small mercy of giving him the night to stew in his own failure.

"Ladies and gentlemen," he addressed the jurors, "we will adjourn for the day and reconvene tomorrow morning at nine a.m. Please be in the jury room no later than eight-forty-five. Thank you and have a good evening."

Findlay didn't offer the same felicitations to Brunelle. He simply left the bench after the jurors had exited the courtroom, leaving the lawyers alone with each other. And with the murderer and his victim's parents.

"We're fucked," Carlisle observed.

Brunelle nodded. "I can't disagree. Any ideas?"

Carlisle frowned and stole a glance at the Pangs who were already standing and waiting to ask them what the heck had just happened. "Take his deal?" she suggested.

Brunelle frowned and looked over at Kincaid. He was smiling ear to ear and slapping Edwards on the back, literally.

"I'm guessing," Brunelle said. "it may be too late for that."

CHAPTER 40

It was over. The trial, his career, everything.

Brunelle should have said something before. But he damn well better say something now. He called Emory and changed their plans. They would meet at his office at 5:00. Carlisle would be there too. He needed to tell them both something.

It went about as well as he'd expected.

"You did what?!" Emory shrieked. "Are you crazy? It's one case. How could you quit over one case?"

Carlisle was quieter, seated opposite him while Emory paced the floor. But she wasn't any less upset. "Why didn't you tell me, Dave? I was right there when you walked out of his office. I thought we were partners."

"We are," Brunelle insisted.

"And I thought you weren't an idiot," Emory added.

"I'm not," Brunelle defended. Then he let his shoulders drop. "Or maybe I am. I didn't see that problem with the search warrant. And now we're screwed."

"You're screwed," Carlisle said. "I'm just going to lose a case. You're going to lose your job."

"Your career," Emory corrected. "How long have you been doing this, Dave? Twenty years? More?"

"I don't really want to think about that right now," he said.

"Well, you better," Emory scoffed, "because you're about to have to start all over again." She looked to Carlisle. "Is it really as bad as all that? Are you definitely going to lose?"

"Oh, yeah," Carlisle nodded profusely. "We're definitely going to lose. We now have zero evidence tying Kincaid to Stephanie Pang's murder. As soon as we rest, Edwards will make a halftime motion to dismiss that count and there's no way Findlay doesn't grant it."

"No, he won't grant it," Brunelle disagreed. "If he dismisses a case, we can appeal his ruling. He'll let it go to the jury, and they'll acquit. We can't appeal an acquittal."

Carlisle looked up at Emory and pointed to Brunelle. "Yes. That. So, yeah, we're definitely going to lose. And in the worst possible way."

"Did you tell anyone?" Emory asked.

Brunelle hesitated. This wasn't going to help matters. "I told Chen."

"Are you fucking kidding me?" Emory and Carlisle both said in unison.

"Chen?" Emory said. "Why, because he has a dick?"

"Because he's my friend," Brunelle defended.

Emory's eyebrows shot up, and she crossed her arms. "I'm not?"

"As your attorney, Mr. Brunelle," Carlisle joked, "I would advise you to shut the hell up."

"What did Chen say?" Emory demanded.

"He said I should tell you," Brunelle admitted.

"He was right," Emory said.

"And he said I was going to screw this up," he added, gesturing back and forth between them. "He knows me pretty well."

Emory uncrossed her arms. "You didn't screw this up, Dave. But damn, you're going to if you won't trust me with stuff like this."

"Also, don't threaten to quit over one case," Carlisle suggested.

Emory shook her head, then lowered it into her hands. After a moment, she looked up again. "God, Dave. What are you going to do?"

Brunelle frowned and let his eyes drop to the floor. "I don't know," he admitted. "Pray for a miracle, I guess."

CHAPTER 41

Miracles were few and far between. That's why they were miracles. But trial work was always filled with the unexpected, so Brunelle had managed to convince himself by the next morning that maybe that horse might talk again.

Carlisle responded to his unjustified optimism by telling him she wished she'd never told him that story.

Once everyone was assembled in the courtroom again, Judge Findlay looked down at the prosecutors. "Any further witnesses?"

Brunelle stood up. It was his case. He'd fall on the sword. "No further witnesses, Your Honor. The State rests."

Findlay turned to Edwards. Normally a judge might ask a defense attorney at that point whether they intended to put on any evidence. Instead, Findlay knew they weren't quite there yet. "You have a motion, I expect, Ms. Edwards?"

Edwards stood. "I do, Your Honor."

And with that the bailiff escorted the jury back out of the courtroom again. In fact, he hadn't left his post by the jury room door, knowing the jurors would be marched in to hear the State rest its case and then be immediately banished again for the defense's halftime motion.

Once the door to the jury room clicked behind the last juror, Judge Findlay nodded to Edwards. "Go ahead, counsel."

"Thank you, Your Honor," Edwards said. "At this time, the defense would move to dismiss the charge against Mr. Kincaid for the murder of Stephanie Pang."

Brunelle could feel the panicked stares of the Pangs on the back of his neck, but he didn't turn around to face them. He would have, if he could have told them everything was going to be all right. But that wasn't true, so he kept his focus on the proceedings in front of him.

"The State has failed to present prima facie evidence connecting my client to the murder of Stephanie Pang," Edwards continued. "Their entire case was based on an alleged DNA match between Ms. Pang and some blood droplets from the trunk of my client's car. But the Court suppressed those droplets and the resultant DNA testing. That left no evidence at all connecting that crime to my client. Accordingly, the Court should dismiss the case. Thank you."

It was a short argument, but that was because it was simple. And every lawyer in the room understood and expected it.

Findlay turned to the prosecution table. "Response?"

"You sure you don't want to do this?" Brunelle tried one more time to get Carlisle to argue the response, but she shook her head.

"It's your career on the line," she answered. "No way I want you looking back ten years from now and blaming me for losing this argument."

Fair enough, Brunelle supposed. He stood up to address

the Court. His only hope was right that Findlay wanted the jury to dismiss the charges through a non-appealable acquittal, rather than do the deed himself.

"Thank you, Your Honor," he started. "As the Court knows, when ruling on a halftime motion to dismiss for insufficient evidence, the Court is to assume the truth of the State's evidence and draw any and all reasonable inferences in favor of the State. I will concede that our case would have been stronger if the Court had not suppressed the DNA evidence, but there is still enough other evidence to allow the case to go to the jury. We have linked the defendant to the murder of Ashleigh Engel, through the license plate observed on the vehicle that was used to dispose of her body. Using *modus operandi* evidence, specifically the proximity of the body disposal sites and the method of killing, the jury could extrapolate that the same person committed both of these murders. Having proved it was the same person and having proved that the defendant committed one of them, the jury could and should be allowed to conclude that the defendant committed both of them. Therefore, viewing the evidence in the light most favorable to the State, a jury could find the defendant guilty of the murder of Stephanie Pang. I'm not saying they will, but I am saying they should be allowed to make that decision. We would ask the Court to deny the motion to dismiss. Thank you."

It was as good an argument as anyone could have made under the circumstances. But it wasn't likely to be enough.

Findlay frowned down at the attorneys. All of them. "I must say, I am very disappointed in the manner in which this case has been tried," he scolded. "Sloppy search warrants, baseless objections, and an attorney I shouldn't have even bothered introducing to the jurors at the beginning of trial."

Everyone looked over at Saxby, who couldn't help the flush that rose up his collar and onto his cheeks.

"I was a trial lawyer for over thirty years," Findlay went on, "and rarely have I seen such a weak case make it so far. I would be well within my rights to terminate the charge involving Stephanie Pang. No appellate court would overturn me based on the record made at this trial."

Brunelle frowned. That was probably true.

"But if I learned one thing in my thirty years as a trial lawyer," Findlay went on, "it was that there's nothing worse than a judge who thinks he's one of the litigants. My job is to resolve disputes. Your job is to try the case. Your job is to convince the jury to render the verdict favorable to you and your client. If I step in the way of that, I forget my role, and prevent both you from performing yours and the jury from performing theirs."

Brunelle let that spark of hope in his chest glow a little brighter. It wasn't a miracle, but it was still something positive.

"I don't believe the jury will convict Mr. Kincaid of the murder of Stephanie Pang," Findlay opined, "but it would be wrong of me to take that decision away from them. Combined with the evidence put on by the State regarding the murder of Ashleigh Engel, there is just barely enough to allow both charges to go to the jury. So, I am denying the motion to dismiss."

Edwards looked crestfallen. She had really expected to win her motion.

"And counsel," Findlay addressed her, "I am going to consider your motion to sever properly re-raised as required to preserve for the appeal. Given the manner in which the evidence has proceeded and the necessity of each case to support the other, I am denying that motion as well."

Edwards just nodded. She seemed unsure what to say. But then her strength seemed to return to her, probably because she realized how terrible the State's case-in-chief had turned out.

"Thank you, Your Honor," she responded respectfully. "I am confident the jury will make the right decision."

Findlay nodded in agreement. "Do you plan to put on any evidence, Ms. Edwards? Or shall I call the jury out just so you can rest in front of them?"

And that's when the miracle happened.

Before Edwards could confirm she wasn't going to call any witnesses, Kincaid grabbed the sleeve of her jacket and tugged on it, hard. She leaned down for him to whisper something in her ear. Brunelle watched as her face blanched, and she began shaking her head strenuously.

"Ms. Edwards?" Judge Findlay inquired. "Is everything okay?"

Edwards raised an index finger to the judge. "Um, I need a moment to speak with my client, Your Honor."

"Of course," Findlay acceded. "However long you need, Ms. Edwards."

What followed was a frenzied, hushed, and very clearly confrontational whispered argument between Edwards and Kincaid, with Saxby nodding in agreement to everything Edwards said.

"What do you think is going on?" Carlisle whispered to Brunelle.

"I think it might be that miracle I prayed for," Brunelle answered hopefully.

"Did you really pray?" Carlisle asked.

"No," Brunelle admitted. "But the Lord helps those who don't ask for help."

"That's not—" Carlisle started. "You just made that up."

Brunelle nodded. "I sure did. Let's hope I'm right."

Edwards finally stood up and addressed Judge Findlay. "I believe we have a problem, Your Honor."

"See?" Brunelle whispered. "Miracle."

"What's the problem?" Findlay asked, his voice deepening as he drew out the words. No judge wants to hear there's a problem when the case is almost over.

"My client wishes to testify," Edwards explained. "Against my advice."

Findlay nodded slowly. "Well, as I recall, that's his decision to make, not yours. He is allowed to disregard your advice."

"Thank you, Your Honor," Kincaid broke protocol by standing up and addressing the judge directly. "I think it is vital that I tell the jury myself that I did not commit these murders."

Findlay pointed a stern finger at Kincaid. "You would do well to sit down and let your attorney do the talking, Mr. Kincaid. I do not want to hear from you, and it is not in your interest to speak without consulting your attorney. I can promise you that."

"So, now you can see my dilemma, Your Honor," Edwards continued. "The problem is not that Mr. Kincaid wishes to disregard my advice to not testify. The problem is that he wishes to testify in a way I know to be untruthful, and I am ethically prohibited from knowingly suborning perjury. If he persists in his desire to testify, I will need to withdraw from the case."

"Which will cause a mistrial," Findlay finished her

thought.

A mistrial would mean having to start the entire case over with a new defense attorney. Brunelle looked to Carlisle, who was looking right back at him.

"Do we want a mistrial?" she asked.

"I'm not sure," Brunelle admitted.

Mistrials were generally considered a win for the defense. Anything that wasn't a conviction was a win for the defense. The only possible advantage to the prosecution was they might get a chance for the case to go better, but even that was unlikely. Findlay's rulings would all still stand—including the suppression of the DNA evidence in the Pang murder. In fact, he would probably go ahead and dismiss that case after all if there wasn't a jury to sanitize the dismissal for him. Even if he didn't, they wouldn't be allowed to even mention the evidence in their opening statement like they had in this trial. This time, they'd had a good faith belief the evidence would be admitted. Next time, not so much. This jury had at least heard from Carlisle that there was a DNA match. They had also heard Edwards object right before they got to that evidence and suddenly no further mention of it. They may have been bland, but they weren't idiots. And the reason the judge would tell them at the end of the trial that anything said by the attorneys should be disregarded if not supported by the evidence was exactly because they were not going to do that. They were going to remember the defense attorney blocked them from seeing the DNA match the prosecutor told them about. This was the only jury who would have that little fact in the backs of their heads.

"No," Brunelle decided, "we don't want a mistrial."

He stood up. "May I be heard on this point, Your Honor?"

Findlay raised an eyebrow at Brunelle. "The prosecutor wants to be heard on the ethical quandary facing the defense attorney?"

"The prosecutor wants to be heard on the possibility of declaring a mistrial in a double murder case," Brunelle responded. "Although, yes, to do that, I would touch on that ethical quandary you mentioned."

Findlay's eyebrows lowered a bit, but knitted together. "All right, Mr. Brunelle. Explain to me how Ms. Edwards can continue to represent Mr. Kincaid if, in so doing, Mr. Kincaid asks her to knowingly suborn perjury."

"I think the key word there is 'knowingly'," Brunelle answered. "Ms. Edwards is concluding that Mr. Kincaid's assertion that he didn't commit the murders is untrue because he repeatedly told her, and me, and Detective Chen, that not only had he committed these murders, but dozens more. However, those statements were made in an effort to negotiate a plea bargain that would have resulted in a lower sentence in exchange for information regarding those other murders. All of that would seem to suggest that he is guilty, and it would be suborning perjury to put him on the stand to say otherwise."

"Yes," Findlay agreed. "It would. Is there more?"

"There is, Your Honor," Brunelle replied. "The key to this analysis is the fact that, in reality, we lawyers don't really know what happened in any of the cases we represent. Not truly. That's why we're the lawyers, not witnesses. Stepping on the occasional skeleton notwithstanding, we aren't there when the crime happens. We don't really know. And that being the case, we can't really know if what our client is telling us is the truth, even when he seems to change his story. Especially when he changes his story."

Findlay's eyebrows were unknitting and raising again. Brunelle didn't know if that was good or bad. He went on regardless.

"Is Mr. Kincaid lying now when he says he didn't commit these murders?" he asked. "Or was he lying before when he told us he committed the murders to get a more lenient sentence? Who knows? Only Mr. Kincaid. But not me, because I wasn't there. And not Ms. Edwards because she wasn't there either. So, that means she can put Mr. Kincaid on the stand, as is his wish and his right, and ask him the questions he wants asked, all without knowingly suborning perjury. And what's more, I am still prohibited by the evidence rules from introducing statements made in plea negotiations, so he'll be able to deny the murders without me bringing up anything he said in those discussions."

Findlay pursed his lips at Brunelle. He wasn't buying it. But he knew he wasn't the one who needed to be buying it. "Ms. Edwards? What do you think of all that?"

Before Edwards could reply, Brunelle whispered over to her. "You don't want a mistrial, Jess. The case couldn't have gone any better for you. You know I'll do everything I can to get that DNA in at the next trial. I might not, but I might. The only trial where it's definitely out is this one. And you have my word, I won't try to introduce anything he said during those plea bargain sessions."

Edwards stared at Brunelle for a few minutes. She wasn't stupid. She knew he wouldn't be making the argument he was making if he didn't also want to avoid a mistrial. But she also knew he had a point. And she knew she could trust his word.

"May I have another moment with my client, Your Honor?" she asked.

"Of course," Findlay agreed.

Another hushed and heated exchange. More nods from Saxby. Then a decision from Edwards. "The defense is ready to proceed, Your Honor. We are not moving for a mistrial. We will be calling Mr. Kincaid to the stand. We're ready for the jury."

"A miracle," Carlisle whispered, shaking her head.

"God bless us, every one," Brunelle whispered back.

Findlay nodded slowly, a bit to Edwards but mostly to himself. He made no effort to disguise his disbelief in this latest turn of events. Then he gathered himself again and nodded to his bailiff. "Bring in the jury."

CHAPTER 42

The jury filed back into the courtroom and took their seats. Then Judge Findlay gazed down at Edwards and asked a question they had already agreed on the answer for.

"Does the defense wish to put on any evidence?"

Edwards stood up. "Yes, Your Honor. The defense calls Michael James Kincaid to the stand."

It was an electric moment. Everyone kind of assumes a defendant probably committed the crime he's charged with. That's why the law requires a presumption of innocence—it wouldn't happen otherwise. So, there's also an expectation that the defendant won't take the stand to deny it—because he did it. Which, Brunelle had to admit, was Kincaid's entire point in wanting to testify. He wanted them to hear him say he didn't do it because he knew they wanted to hear him say it too.

Kincaid stood up and shimmied behind Saxby's chair to be able to make his way to the witness stand. If the jurors hadn't already figured out why the three corrections officers were there the entire trial, they would have realized it when all of them took several steps toward him to discourage any thoughts of making a break for it. But Kincaid was smarter than that. Or at least he thought he was.

Edwards waited for Findlay to swear her client in like any other witness and for him to take his seat on the witness stand. She couldn't keep him off the stand, but she could limit his time on it.

"Please state your name for the record," she started.

Kincaid turned to the jury—he'd learned from the State's witnesses—and smiled broadly. It wasn't as charming as he probably thought it was. "Michael James Kincaid."

Edwards didn't waste time with his employment or education or experience. None of that was relevant. He wanted to deny the murders. Fine.

"Did you kill Ashleigh Engel?"

Kincaid shifted his expression to one of concern. He frowned and shook his head sadly. "No," he assured the jurors.

"Did you kill Stephanie Pang?"

His concern deepened. He shook his head again, for a half second longer. "No. No, I did not."

Edwards looked up to Findlay. "No further questions." Then she marched back to her seat.

Kincaid looked surprised by her sudden departure. No doubt he had hoped for the opportunity to explain away all the State's evidence—what there was of it. But not to worry. Brunelle had something else he could try to explain away.

Brunelle stood up. Kincaid was his witness. It was his case. His career. Everything sends a subtle signal. Saxby had done zero. Carlisle had done about 50%. But this was his. And if he was going down, he wanted everyone to know why.

He approached Kincaid slowly. If it had been electric when Kincaid took the stand, it was thermonuclear as Brunelle approached the witness stand. There was nothing more dramatic in the law than the prosecutor confronting the defendant. Good versus evil. Right versus wrong. Justice versus murder.

He pulled a piece of paper from his jacket pocket. He'd been carrying it in his pocket every single day of trial. A reminder of why he was fighting so hard with so little. He shoved it at Kincaid. "Read this."

Kincaid hesitated.

"I need to object, Your Honor," Edwards interrupted. She stood up to address the judge. "I don't even know what that document is. I'd like to see it first."

"It's a poem," Brunelle answered her directly. "And I think you've seen it before. You quoted it in your opening statement."

Edwards went pale.

"You quoted it, Jess," Brunelle repeated, shaking the piece of paper. "You knew about this."

"Do you want to see the document, Ms. Edwards?" Judge Findlay interjected.

Edwards took a moment, then shook her head and sat down again. "No, Your Honor. I believe Mr. Brunelle is correct."

Brunelle turned back to Kincaid. "Read it."

"Is that a question?" Kincaid tried to deflect.

"It's a directive," Brunelle replied. "Read it."

Kincaid laughed nervously and looked up at the judge. "Do I have to respond if it's not a question?"

Findlay looked down at Brunelle. He could have asked to see the document himself. He could have instructed Brunelle to lay further foundation. He could have told Brunelle to ask a question. Instead, he turned a steel eyed gaze to Kincaid. "Read it."

Kincaid laughed nervously again, but less so. He took the paper from Brunelle and squinted at it. "The writing is rather small…"

"Read it, Kincaid," Brunelle growled. "Nice and loud so everyone can hear it."

Kincaid cleared his throat and looked at Edwards for help. She offered none. Findlay was still glaring down at him. Brunelle wasn't budging either.

"Yes, okay…" Kincaid stammered. "When the verdicts are read…"

"Louder," Brunelle instructed.

Kincaid narrowed his eyes at Brunelle. "You know what? I'm afraid I'm not able to make this out. It's in pencil, and the writing is smudged, and my eyes aren't what they used to be."

"Brunelle snatched it from Kincaid's hands and turned to read it to the jury:

When the verdicts are read,
'Not Guilty' times two,
I'll do it again,
And it's all thanks to you.

He turned back to Kincaid. "Your words."

"You read them," Kincaid pointed out.

"You mailed this to me just before the trial began, didn't you?"

Kincaid shifted in his seat. His eyes darted around the courtroom again. Beads of sweat popped onto his flushed, bald head. "No," he claimed.

But no one believed him.

And that was good enough for Brunelle.

"No further questions."

Judge Findlay asked Edwards if she had any redirect examination, but of course she said no, and Kincaid was allowed to return to his seat next to her but as good as a million miles away.

"Any further witnesses from the defense?" Findlay asked, as a matter of course.

Edwards stood up. "No, Your Honor. The defense rests."

CHAPTER 43

It was all over but the crying. And the closing arguments. And before that, the judge reading the jury instructions. And the verdict. So, it wasn't really over after all. But it was almost over.

Carlisle gave the opening; that meant Brunelle gave the closing. Once Findlay had finished reading the instructions—statements of law to guide the jurors in their deliberations—it was time. The courtroom was packed again. All the same people as for the opening. No pressure.

"Ladies and gentlemen," Judge Findlay announced, "please give your attention to Mr. Brunelle, who will deliver closing argument on behalf of the State."

Brunelle stood up and made his way to that sweet spot in front of the jury. He wasn't going for the theatrics of standing in front of the defense table and pointing at the defendant. He just wanted to wrap it up and hope for the best.

One of the biggest mistakes trial attorneys made was forgetting the jury had seen all the same evidence the lawyer was about to summarize. The only thing worse than being forced to listen to a terribly told story was to have to sit there while someone repeated the entire story from the beginning. Lawyers could think a lot of themselves. And lawyers liked to talk. It was the main thing they did. So, some lawyers would actually brag about how many hours their closing arguments were, totally oblivious to the fact that their jurors were somewhere else right then complaining about that lawyer who just wouldn't shut up.

The dangers were even higher for a prosecutor. Most criminal convictions reversed by the appellate courts were overturned because of misconduct by the prosecutor in closing argument. Every other lawyer was allowed to bring all of their advocacy skills to bear in closing arguments. But not prosecutors. Defendants had too many rights that might be infringed on by unfettered arguments of a prosecutor. The prosecutor's job wasn't to win the case; it was to seek justice. A conviction in violation of a defendant's rights wasn't just.

The best advice Brunelle ever got, at least about closing argument, was to get over himself. 'The jury knows what they heard. The only thing you can do in closing is get the case reversed.'

So, Brunelle clasped those earnest hands in front of himself and started.

"The defendant murdered Stephanie Pang and dumped her body behind an abandoned business no one even remembers the name of anymore. The defendant murdered Ashleigh Engel and dumped her body a few hundred yards north of Stephanie's body, behind the abandoned PetMax warehouse. And none of us would have known that if it weren't for a hungry Doberman named Ginger."

He paused. Pauses were important, sometimes more

important than words. But his was mostly just because it had been a long trial, and the weight of the pending verdict, with all of its implications, was heavy on his shoulders.

"You've heard all the evidence," he continued. "You've watched the video. You've seen the stills of the license plate. You've heard how similar the murders were. You know he did it, even if the evidence is circumstantial, even if we don't have the murders on video. You know he did it, and that's enough. It has to be."

Another pause, and a look over his shoulder at Kincaid after all.

"It has to be," he repeated, "because you also know what will happen if he gets away with these. Don't take my word for it. Take his. He told you himself. Well, he told me, but you got to hear it too. When the verdicts are read, 'Not Guilty' times two, he'll do it again, and it's all thanks," a final pause, and a finger pointed, not at himself, but directly at the jurors, "to you."

That was it. There wasn't more to say that really needed to be said. They knew the evidence. They knew he was guilty. They knew what would happen if they acquitted him. Brunelle would just have to hope they did the right thing.

"Ladies and gentlemen of the jury, I'm asking you—" He glanced at Carlisle, and the Pangs sitting behind her, "We're asking you to return verdicts of guilty to both counts. Guilty to the murder of Ashleigh Engel, and guilty to the murder of Stephanie Pang. Thank you."

And with that, they were finished. There was nothing more they could do, except hope it had been enough.

Brunelle sat down next to Carlisle. She didn't say, 'Good job.' He didn't feel like he deserved it anyway. They both just trained their attention on Edwards as she rose and approached the jury box herself.

"Now, ladies and gentlemen," Judge Findlay announced, "please give your attention to Ms. Edwards who will deliver closing argument on behalf of the defense."

Edwards took her place before the jury box. She wasn't nearly as casual as she appeared for her opening statement. If anything, her expression seemed angry. Brunelle wasn't sure at who, though. Him? Findlay? Kincaid? Herself? Probably all of the above. And maybe more.

"When you first came into this courtroom," she began, "the judge told you two things. One, my client was charged with two counts of murder in the first degree; and two, he was presumed innocent of those charges. Each and every one of you swore an oath to presume him innocent unless and unless and until the State presented to you proof beyond a reasonable doubt. Even though he was charged with not one murder but two. *Especially* because he was charged with not one murder but two."

Yes, definitely angry. She wasn't quite shouting at the jurors, but she did seem to be scolding them.

"The biggest danger in a case like this," she waved vaguely around the courtroom, "is that the jury will turn off their ears as soon as they hear the word 'murder', let alone two counts of murder. The burden of proof is the same for shoplifting as it is for murder, but not really. It's supposed to be, but we all know—or at least we all fear—juries don't really treat them the same. If you acquit a shoplifter, but he really did it, so what? But an accused murderer? No way. No way you risk letting him off. Even less so if he might be a double murderer."

Edwards shook her head, as if answering her own

question.

"And so, that's this case. Because quite frankly, the State didn't even come close to proving these charges beyond a reasonable doubt. They didn't prove them by a preponderance of the evidence. I would submit to you they didn't even establish probable cause, the lowest standard."

Brunelle was glad to hear Edwards listing off legal standards. Juries didn't know the different burdens of proof for different types of proceedings. It meant losing the jurors, even if just for a few seconds, which was good for his side.

"Here's what they told you." Edwards counted off on her fingers. "One, two women were murdered. Two, their bodies were found really close to each other. Three, a so-called forensic entomologist—a bug expert—guessed when one of the women was probably dumped, if he got the species right, and the weather, and the temperature, and God knows what else. Four, a car was seen driving away from one of the dump sites at roughly the same time the bug guy guessed the body was dumped. Five, the license plate might have been my client's, *if* that eight was a B and that H was a K and that four was an A."

She held up one hand, fingers extended.

"That's it," she said. "That's all they gave you. That is not proof beyond a reasonable doubt. That's not proof of anything. That's proof that a car with a similar license plate to my client's car drove by in the same week that someone left a dead body there. I mean, they didn't even prove the person who dumped the body was the one who actually killed her. Maybe it was someone who found the body somewhere else and decided to move it for some unknown reason. I don't know. Do you? No, you don't. And if you don't know, you can't convict."

She was definitely scolding the jurors. And no one liked

to be scolded.

"That's it," she repeated. "You can't convict. Not if you care about the oath you took. Not if you care about our criminal justice system. Not if you care about the presumption of innocence and proof beyond a reasonable doubt."

She turned and pointed at Kincaid. "Don't ask yourself, 'Did he do it?'" She swung her arm to point at Brunelle and Carlisle. "Ask yourself, 'Did they prove it?' And if the answer is no, then your answer is 'Not Guilty'. And yes," a glower directly at Brunelle, "not guilty times two."

With that, Edwards turned around and trudged back to her seat without so much as a concluding 'Thank you'. She just sat down and glued her eyes to the judge, ignoring the jurors, the prosecutors, even her own client. And definitely Peter Saxby.

Judge Findlay waited a moment, just to make sure both sides were really finally done talking, then he addressed the jurors one last time. "Ladies and gentlemen, that concludes the closing arguments. You are now excused to the jury room to begin your deliberations."

The jurors knew the drill by then. They stood up and followed the bailiff into the jury room.

Everyone, including Brunelle and Carlisle, stood up as they exited, the same respect afforded judges when they entered and exited the courtroom.

"What do you think?" Brunelle whispered to Carlisle as the jury room door closed.

"I think you're both right," Carlisle answered with a gesture toward Edwards. "You didn't really prove it, but they know he did it."

"Damn," Brunelle hissed. "Doesn't that mean an

acquittal?"

"I hope not," Carlisle answered. "Otherwise, my next case might be against you."

CHAPTER 44

After the rush of the trial came the agony of waiting on the verdict. These particular verdicts were taking days. Three full days after closing arguments and still nothing from the jurors. Brunelle knew that wasn't good. Long deliberations were rarely good for the prosecution. The quicker the verdict, the more certain they were, and that was usually because the evidence was overwhelming. Here, it was the opposite of that. So, maybe it was good news after all. They hadn't acquitted yet.

It was the fourth day of deliberations just before lunch, when Brunelle finally got the call from the bailiff. "The jury has reached a verdict."

The words every trial lawyer loves and hates.

"We will convene at one o'clock to receive the verdict," the bailiff continued.

Even worse. There was no way Brunelle was going to be able to eat while waiting to hear what the verdict was. "Thanks. I'll let Ms. Carlisle know."

"No need," the bailiff replied. "I called her first."

Brunelle held the receiver for a moment before hanging up. Carlisle was already in his doorway.

"He called you first," Brunelle said when he turned around and noticed her.

"Maybe he knows something we don't," she said. Then she gazed around his office with an approving nod. "Can I have your office if we lose?"

"Can you shut the hell up?" Brunelle returned. "Don't jinx the verdict."

"Superstitious much?" Carlisle teased.

He knocked on his faux wood veneered desk. "Anything, if it helps us get the right verdict."

CHAPTER 45

Everyone was there, and well before one o'clock. Edwards and Saxby, of course. And Kincaid, looking confident again, more so than Brunelle thought he should have. Chen, the Pangs, Emory. Even some of the detectives from their big meeting. And sneaking in at the last second, even as Findlay was taking the bench and everyone was ordered to stand to herald the judge's arrival, Duncan. Brunelle saw him duck in and head to the back of the courtroom. He sighed and returned his attention to the judge.

"This morning at approximately eleven-forty-five, the presiding juror informed the bailiff the jury had reached a verdict," Findlay announced, a bit unnecessarily, since everyone was there precisely because they knew the jury had reached a verdict. "Bailiff, bring in the jury."

The bailiff stood up from his seat below the judge and marched across the courtroom to open the jury room door. It was all very formal. All very time-consuming. Hadn't they gotten to the point, Brunelle wished, where the jury could just send a group text of a thumbs-up or thumbs-down emoji? Every second of waiting was agony piled upon the agony of the previous second.

Finally, the jury room door opened and in came the jurors. Trial lawyers will tell you there are tricks to reading the jurors' faces. If they look at the defendant, it's an acquittal, but if they look away it's a conviction. Watch to see who's holding the verdict form because that's the presiding juror and you can try to remember whether they were more pro-defense or pro-prosecution during jury selection. Brunelle had tried enough cases to know those tricks were worthless. Short of the jurors giving one side or the other a wink and a thumbs-up, there was nothing the lawyers could do except wait as the formality ground on.

"Will the presiding juror please stand?" Findlay requested as soon as everyone in the courtroom sat down.

An older woman in the front row stood up, her short white hair and white pearls matching the white of the verdict forms she held in wrinkled, liver spotted hands.

"Has the jury reached a verdict?" Findlay asked her.

"Yes, Your Honor," the presiding juror answered, holding up the verdict forms a bit higher.

"Please hand the verdict forms to the bailiff," Judge Findlay instructed.

She did as she was directed, and the bailiff marched the verdict forms across the courtroom to hand to the judge. Brunelle watched him to see if he stole a glance of the results—Brunelle would have if he'd been the bailiff—but it looked like he simply transported them without any attempt to glean their content.

Judge Findlay accepted the verdict forms, then took a moment to read them. His face was as inscrutable as the bailiff's or the presiding juror's. They all knew the verdict. The only ones who didn't were the ones who fought the case for them.

"Will the defendant please rise," Findlay instructed.

Kincaid stood up, looking as confident as ever. But Brunelle could see those beads of sweat at his temple again. Edwards stood up with him, and after a moment, Saxby too.

It was finally time to learn whether they should have accepted Kincaid's offer after all.

"Verdict Form Number One," Findlay read the verdict aloud. "In the matter of *The State of Washington versus Michael James Kincaid*, we, the jury, find the defendant..."

Please, please, please, Brunelle was thinking. He knew Edwards was thinking the same thing.

"... guilty of the murder in the first degree of Ashley Engel."

A wave of relief flooded over Brunelle. Carlisle was ecstatic, but Brunelle was simply relieved. He'd been right.

"Verdict Form Number Two," Findlay continued to read, over the gasps and hoots of the gallery. "We find the defendant not guilty of the murder in the first degree of Stephanie Pang."

Oh no, Brunelle thought. He'd almost forgotten about that in the relief of getting the conviction for the first count. It wasn't a win. It was a tie.

For him anyway. For Arnold and Eleanor Pang, it was a loss. Eleanor began to wail uncontrollably. Arnold tried to comfort her, but there was no comfort from injustice.

Brunelle looked over to Kincaid. He wanted Kincaid to feel like it was a loss. But he was just standing there, waiting for

Brunelle to look at him. They locked eyes. But Kincaid's twitched and Brunelle knew he'd won just enough—twenty years minimum, thirty years maximum—to claim the victory.

EPILOGUE

Findlay sentenced Kincaid to the high end, thirty years. Kincaid would have to make it to eighty-one to get out again. It was unlikely to happen, and if it did, at that age, after three decades in prison, Kincaid wouldn't be a threat to anyone anymore.

The Pangs were ultimately okay with the result, in large part because they got to see their daughter's murderer sentenced to die (probably) in prison. It didn't really matter whose name was on the verdict form with the word 'guilty' on it.

Edwards wasn't nearly as bitter about the result as Brunelle had expected. She'd done all she could and actually notched a 'not guilty' verdict on a Murder One case, all thanks to her legal skills in spotting and arguing the search warrant issue.

Carlisle was satisfied with the verdict. She would have preferred two 'Guilty's but, as she explained to everyone who would listen, Brunelle insisted on arguing the search warrant issue himself.

And Duncan. Duncan was still upset with Brunelle. Despite the verdicts, Brunelle had dismissed him, misled him, and threatened him. That wasn't how a boss should be treated. The remedy lay either with Brunelle changing his ways, or Duncan terminating their employee-boss relationship.

"You lost the Pang case," Duncan said when they met later in his office.

"But I won the Engel case," Brunelle pointed out. "Tie goes to the runner, right?"

"Are you sure you're the runner?" Duncan asked. "And I'm more of a poker man than a baseball man. Tie goes to the house. And I'm definitely the house."

Brunelle grimaced at the analogy and nodded. "You're right, Matt. I told you I'd win the cases, but I didn't. Not quite. Not both of them. I just want you to know, it's been an honor working for you. I'll never forget the opportunities you gave me, or the guidance, or the friendship. I'm sorry I let you down."

Duncan nodded back at Brunelle. "Are you done?"

Brunelle cocked his head. "Done?"

"Done telling me how great I am," Duncan explained. "I mean, I know it. There aren't a lot of bosses who would put up with your crap. But I don't mind hearing it if you want to go on."

"Uh," Brunelle hesitated. "Should I?"

Duncan laughed. "You mean, do you need to kiss up to me to keep your job? No. You don't need to do that. I'm not accepting your resignation. I never was going to. That would be crazy. But I thought it might motivate you if you really thought you were gonna lose your entire career."

Brunelle just blinked at his boss for several seconds. "Are you fucking kidding me? I thought... I was ready... I almost lost my girlfriend over this."

Duncan laughed again. "I bet that was more on you than on me, if I know you, which I do."

Brunelle opened his mouth to argue, but then closed it again. Duncan did know him.

"But I will tell you this, and in all seriousness," Duncan went on. "You're not fired, but I think you could do with a break. When was the last time you took a vacation?"

Brunelle thought for a moment. "I'm not sure."

"Then it's been too long." Duncan got up out of his chair and walked over to put an arm around Brunelle. "I want you to take a leave of absence. Just a month. But get out of here. Take that girlfriend of yours someplace nice and try to make up for however you made this bad situation even worse."

"Are you serious right now?" Brunelle asked.

"Deathly serious," Duncan answered. "And I use that word intentionally. You need a break from death. Go live a little. When you get back, I'll be happy to assign you to the worst, most terrible murder case we have going. Deal?"

Brunelle hesitated. He'd been doing homicides for so long he couldn't imagine taking that much time away from the constant drumbeat of murder and death. Or rather, he could imagine it; he'd been forced to. And he was worried he wouldn't be able to come back to it all.

But he shook Duncan's hand anyway. "Deal."

THE END

THE DAVID BRUNELLE LEGAL THRILLERS
Presumption of Innocence
Tribal Court
By Reason of Insanity
A Prosecutor for the Defense
Substantial Risk
Corpus Delicti
Accomplice Liability
A Lack of Motive
Missing Witness
Diminished Capacity
Devil's Plea Bargain

THE TALON WINTER LEGAL THRILLERS
Winter's Law
Winter's Chance
Winter's Reason

ALSO BY STEPHEN PENNER
Scottish Rite
Blood Rite
Last Rite
Mars Station Alpha
The Godling Club

ABOUT THE AUTHOR

Stephen Penner is an attorney, author, and artist from Seattle.

In addition to the *David Brunelle Legal Thriller Series*, he also writes the *Talon Winter Legal Thrillers*, starring Tacoma criminal defense attorney Talon Winter, the *Maggie Devereaux Paranormal Mysteries*, recounting the exploits of an American graduate student in the magical Highlands of Scotland, and several stand-alone works.

For more information, please visit the author's website: *www.stephenpenner.com*.

Manufactured by Amazon.ca
Bolton, ON